"Nick

He captured the image. "Two heartbeats."

"What?" Kirby struggled to her elbow, bewilderment compounding dread and confusing her even more. "You're nowhere near my heart."

"Here." His shaking finger pointed to the fuzzy image. "You're pregnant with twins."

"I'm pregnant?" Pregnant? This wasn't possible—she had the blood work and the letter from a Melbourne specialist to prove it impossible. She blinked three times, but still the image stayed the same. Two tiny embryonic sacs could be clearly seen on the screen.

She sat up quickly, and threw her arms around Nick. "I'm pregnant. I can't believe it.... I never thought it could happen to me. It's a miracle...."

Dear Reader,

Welcome to Port Bathurst! Summer holidays at the beach are a quintessential part of the Australian way of life. Sun, sand, surf and sunscreen go hand in hand with fetes, markets, camping and cricket. Whenever I visit a town I find myself wondering about the residents and what brought them to this particular place, and that is how I dreamed up Kirby and Nick's story.

Nick has faced one of life's toughest challenges, and he's come to Port Bathurst for some R & R before he resumes his big-city life. He has a life plan, and nothing will derail him from that. Kirby had a plan, too, but sometimes life throws a sucker punch. She's run from *her* big-city life with no intention of returning, but her new start hits a brick wall almost from day one.

Neither Nick nor Kirby is looking for love, but they end up finding it under clear blue skies, on white sandy beaches and in a town that reaches out and claims them as its own.

For those of you interested in the places that have influenced the creation of Port Bathurst, they are Mallacoota, Queenscliff, Port Welshpool and Apollo Bay. If you're ever in Victoria, take the drive along the coast from east to west and soak up the glorious scenery that inspired this story.

I also have pictures on my Web site, www.fionalowe.com, so make a cup of tea and have a look. I'd love to see you there!

Love,

Fiona x

MIRACLE: TWIN BABIES

Fiona Lowe

HARLEQUIN®

TORONTO • NEW YORK • LONDON
AMSTERDAM • PARIS • SYDNEY • HAMBURG
STOCKHOLM • ATHENS • TOKYO • MILAN • MADRID
PRAGUE • WARSAW • BUDAPEST • AUCKLAND

ISBN-13: 978-0-373-06702-2

MIRACLE: TWIN BABIES

First North American Publication 2009

This edition published by arrangement with Harlequin Books S.A.

www.eHarlequin.com

Printed in U.S.A.

MIRACLE: TWIN BABIES

To Serena—for her eagle eyes, her hard questions and her enthusiastic support.

Thank you!

CHAPTER ONE

OXYGEN stats are dropping! Tube him!

More blood, he's bleeding out!

Flatlining. Stand clear, now!

A lone kookaburra's raucous laugh vibrated the hot, torpid summer afternoon air, mocking Nick Dennison's thoughts. Thoughts that were firmly fixed in the past, over one and half years ago before everything in his life had gone pear-shaped. Back in a time when being a doctor had defined him and life had been work, and work had been his life.

Resting back on his haunches after being bent over pulling weeds, he pushed against the trowel and stood up, stretching his back. Sweat ran down his cheeks and he wiped his face against the tight sleeve of his T-shirt, leaving a trail of rich black earth against the soft cotton.

Through the shimmer of the eucalypt-oil heat haze he could see in the distance the small fishing town of Port Bathurst, affectionately known by the locals as Port. Snuggled into the curve of white sand and turquoise water, protected on one side by a treacherous reef and on the other side by a granite-flecked mountain, Port was a glorious work of nature and far from the man-made inner-city life he'd always known.

A wet nose nuzzled his ankle as a ball dropped next to his foot. He glanced down at the intelligent and loving eyes of his blue heeler. 'Have you rounded up the chooks yet, Turbo?'

The dog cocked his head to the side, picked up the ball and sat down, hope and expectation clear in his expression.

Nick rubbed the cattle dog's black ears. 'I take it that's a yes.' He accepted the saliva-covered ball and hurled it off into the bracken, watching the dog tear after it. He had once talked to a hundred people a day—now he was conversing with a dog and talking to his vegetables. He'd craved solitude and simplicity for a long time. Now he finally had it.

He heard the phone ringing through the open window of his cottage and instinctively glanced at his watch. Tuesday. Five o'clock. His mother would have just got in from her midweek ladies' tennis match. He let the phone ring out. Being asked a hundred questions about his health and his lack of future plans wasn't conversation.

He grabbed a shovel and started spreading manure, losing himself in the joy of being able to do physical work again, closing his mind to everything except the rhythm of the movement.

Dr Kirby Atherton jogged down the long Port Bathurst pier just as the last tinges of orange faded from the cloud-studded sky. Another hot day was on its way, which would make the holidaymakers visiting town happy, but distress many of her elderly patients. She'd only been in town a few weeks but her early morning run was part of her routine. She lacked control over many things in her life, but keeping fit—*that* she could control. Running both exhausted and exhilarated her and helped keep the demons at bay.

'Morning, Doc.' A wide grin sliced across a weather-beaten face.

Kirby jogged on the spot next to a stack of crayfish pots and looked down at Garry Braithwaite, sluicing his fishing boat. 'Morning, Garry.'

'Everyone calls me Gaz, love.'

She noted his request for next time she greeted him. Acclimatising to Port was a lesson in letting go of city ways and shortening every long name and lengthening every short one. 'Good catch?'

'Not bad.' He indicated a large white plastic trough filled with crawling crustaceans. 'These beauties will be in Japan before you're in bed tonight.'

'That's amazing.' She glanced behind her at the fish co-op which was ablaze with lights. This was its busiest time of day as it accepted the catches of the local fleet. She turned back, a wistful tone in her voice. 'Are they all going to Japan? Not even a few to the farmers' market?'

'Just the ones the co-op rejects. I've got about five.' He started to wind up the hose, his expression cheeky. 'Do you have a special dinner guest tonight, Doc? Perhaps you should talk to Deano and get some abalone.'

Kirby ignored the inference. In some ways coming to Port had been like stepping back in time. It appeared to be the small town's opinion that no matter how qualified, successful or independent a woman was, if she was young and single she must be looking for a husband. A few months ago Kirby might have agreed. 'Save me a small cray, Gaz, and I'll catch you at the market in half an hour.'

She turned and switched on her MP3 player, and with her feet matching the thumping bass beat she ran toward the aroma of freshly brewed coffee, the sweet smell of fruit muffins straight out of the oven and the scent of rich brown earth clinging to freshly picked produce.

She'd been trying to get to the market for the last three Saturdays but each time a sick patient had derailed her plans. Coming to Port was supposed to be the commencement of her GP training but within a week of starting as the town doctor, her mentor had fallen ill. Without supervision, Kirby was flying by the seat of her pants.

It was still early in the season but if the last weeks had been a typical Port Bathurst summer then she really needed some extra help as well as a mentor. She didn't want to have to move again and find another GP programme, and returning to Melbourne was *not* an option. Surely there was an experienced doctor with a family who wanted to have an idyllic summer by the sea?

But Port Bathurst wasn't Lorne or Sorrento, it didn't have designer clothing shops, the mobile phone coverage was intermittent and the dial-up internet was really more down than up. The glory days of it being a gold-rush port had faded. Today it sat at the end of a very long road, with a large chunk of wilderness between it and the nearest town. Although all these things had been part of the charm that had drawn Kirby to the historic town, it seemed to put most people off. No one had answered her advertisement.

Kirby surveyed the slowly building crowd. It was still early so there was a marked absence of teenagers but plenty of empty-nesters clutching well-planned lists, examining the fresh produce and enthusiastically haggling over prices. Toddlers and preschoolers full of energy zipped up and down between stalls, way ahead of their half-asleep parents. A man in his thirties walked past, pride radiating off him as he held his wife's hand and wore a baby sling on his chest, his newborn snuggled against him fast asleep.

Family is everything. She steeled herself against Anthony's uncompromising voice but it wasn't enough to stop the ache that throbbed inside her whenever she glimpsed such a scene. She swallowed against the tightness in her throat, rolled her shoulders back and kept walking. Forget eating healthy—right now she needed hazelnut coffee and a hot jam donut.

She unexpectedly paused, derailed in her quest by the sight of an old wooden trestle table groaning under the weight of bountiful vegetables. Arranged in groups for effect, the vivid colours of nature demanded attention. The red and green skins of the capsicums shone, the plump white ends of spring onions contrasted stunningly with the healthy dark green tails, and the ruby tomatoes promised an old-fashioned, rich flavour. The vividness of the colours astounded her and she was struck by how lush and enticing everything looked. These vegetables glowed with good health and were positively sexy.

'Can I help you?'

The deep voice vibrated the air around her, moving it across her skin like a silk caress and leaving behind a tingling trail of unmet need. Completely stunned by her body's reaction to a disembodied voice, she glanced up.

Emerald-green eyes, the colour of the bay, gazed down at her, swirling with hints of blue and dancing with undiluted charm. An indistinct memory stirred.

'Anything take your fancy?'

You. She bit off the word that thundered hard and fast through her head and found her voice. 'I've never seen vegetables like this before. The colours are amazing.'

He smiled and dimples carved into his cheeks, seeming to darken his early morning stubble. Surprisingly deep lines for a man who looked to be in his early thirties bracketed a wide mouth, and unexpected fine lines radiated from his eyes toward short dark hair streaked with silver. 'Thanks. They're my first crop of organic vegetables so I feel like a proud dad with his children.'

She raised her brows. 'Except you're selling them.'

He grinned. 'Every kid has to go out and make their way in the world.'

She laughed. He was the most gorgeous farmer she'd ever met. Not that he really looked like a farmer despite the fact he had a cattle dog sitting quietly beside him. There was no sign of a battered hat and his pressed stone-coloured shorts contrasted with a fresh blue-and-white-striped short-sleeved shirt—smart, casual weekender clothes, the type that a man of the city would wear. A gym-buffed man of the city.

Working out in a gym could have given him his broad chest and wide shoulders but not the sun-kissed skin. Skin stretched over taut muscles and was covered by a smattering of golden hair which was in stark contrast to his darker head hair. No, this man's body emanated a base power generated by sheer physical hard work.

She studied his face. Something about him seemed familiar and yet nothing about him prompted recognition.

His brilliant green eyes danced at her. 'If you tell me what you're thinking about, perhaps I can suggest a vegetable to match?'

Horrified that he'd caught her out staring at him as if he was on display like his stock, she randomly pointed to a stack of vine-ripened tomatoes. 'I'll take two, please.' She noticed small white scars on the back of his hand as he reached across the table.

Long, tanned fingers picked up the red, round fruit and placed them lightly against her palm. 'I recommend you spread hot, grainy toast with the local goat's cheese in virgin olive oil, and then top it with thin slices of tomato covered with freshly ground pepper and some of my basil. You'll be licking your lips and fingers to soak up every last wondrous morsel.'

An image of him languorously licking her fingers spun through her, making her dizzy. She'd obviously been working way too hard if her mind could just shoot off on dangerous tangents like that. She'd come to Port Bathurst to start over and to protect herself, and that didn't mean melting into a puddle of lust at a stranger's feet.

'Right, thanks. Organic food and recipes, too. Awesome!' *Can you hear yourself? You sound inane.*

He shot her a crooked smile. 'Enjoy. It's the small things in life that are worth holding on to.'

'A farmer *and* a philosopher?'

A shadow flickered across his gaze for a moment before being absorbed by a world-weary smile. 'Something like that. Enjoy your weekend.' He accepted her money and turned to serve his next customer.

A flash of something akin to rejection spiked her, which was illogical and ridiculous. This wasn't a social situation. He was a stallholder and she was a customer and he had a line of customers behind her waiting to be served. *No man is worth it, remember!* Her indignant and wounded subconscious kicked her hard, reminding her of Anthony's betrayal.

Reminding her of why she'd come to Port Bathurst in the first place. A new start—keep moving forward and never look back.

But repeating her mantra didn't stop a deep line of disappointment rolling through her. A disappointment which was completely out of proportion to the situation. Man, she must be tired, but then again, working flat out for a month would do that to a girl. She tucked some flyaway strands of hair behind her ears and took a deep breath. *Just keep moving forward.* She turned and walked toward the coffee cart, needing the java jolt and sweet taste of hazelnut more than ever.

The queue for coffee was long and congenial and she chatted to people about the weather, signed a petition to save the old bridge, and listened to concerns about how the new fishing quotas would affect the town's main industry. Getting to know Port was all part and parcel of being a country GP.

'There you go, Doc. One skinny hazelnut latte, super-sized.'

'Thanks, Jade. It smells divine.' Kirby gripped the cup and headed toward a free table. She put her tomatoes and coffee down and slid into the chair. Carefully easing the tight-fitting plastic lid off the top of the cup, she admired the foamy froth, took a deep anticipatory breath and lifted the coffee to her lips.

The frantic barking of a dog and yelling voices stalled her sip and she turned sharply toward the commotion.

Jake, Gaz's ten-year-old son, came running toward her, his chest heaving and his face pinched and white. 'Dr Kirby, Dad can't breathe!'

She leapt to her feet and yelled out to Jade in the coffee cart, 'Get the St John's kit from the hall.' Then she ran, following the boy back toward his father. The crowd opened up around them, easing their passage through the closely lined stalls. She hurdled some packing cases and in the distance she could see Gaz leaning forward, coughing violently and trying to breathe.

His solid height and weight obscured the person who was helping him. Someone had his right arm around Gaz's waist and his hand pressed firmly against the fisherman's chest. Thankfully someone who obviously knew first aid. Kirby hoped he was giving a sharp blow to Garry's back at chest level.

Kirby ducked around the craft stalls, concentrating on her feet missing cables and desperately wishing for a more direct route to get to her patient. She looked up again. Gaz continued to cough, but his colour was fading from bright red to white.

As she got closer she saw the first-aider was her farmer. He'd just placed both his hands under Garry's armpits and thrust inwards. Surprise washed through her that he knew this newer and less damaging technique. Most first-aiders still used the older Heimlich manoeuvre. She prayed that whatever was choking Garry would be projected out of his mouth soon.

Just as she reached them, Garry slumped forward, his face blue. Instinctively, Kirby threw herself at him, her shoulder catching him on the chest, preventing him from falling. 'I'm—'

'Help me get him down.' The farmer's voice held an unexpected authoritative command and a tone that brooked no argument. 'I'm a doctor, just do as I say.'

Kirby staggered under the unexpected words and Gaz's weight as she tried to grab his arms. A farmer-cum-doctor? But she had no time to think about that strange combination. All her concentration was on the fisherman who struggled for every life-sustaining breath.

'Doctor!' Jade ran up clutching the first-aid backpack which Kirby immediately put on the ground and opened.

'I need the pocket mask,' the doctor and Kirby both said at the same time.

Questioning green eyes framed with thick brown lashes appraised her as she helped him lower Garry onto the ground. 'I'm Kirby Atherton, the town's doctor.'

'Excellent. I'm Nick. Let's get him onto his side and I'll try more lateral chest thrusts.' He knelt next to their patient, placing his hands firmly over the ribcage. Using his weight, he pressed with a downward and forward movement.

'I'll check his airway.' Kirby rolled a now blue Garry onto his side and put her finger inside his mouth, hoping desperately to feel a foreign object.

'Anything?' The word held hope and dread.

'Nothing.' She rolled him back, checked his carotid pulse and chest movements, and called out to Jake. 'What was Dad eating when he started choking?'

The trembling boy tried to speak. 'St-stra-strawberry. He threw it in the air and catched it in his mouth.'

'It will have lodged in his trachea.' Nick voiced her exact thought.

'Starting mouth-to-mouth.' She applied the pocket mask over Garry's mouth and lowered her head. He needed air but she had no idea if she could she manage to force any past the obstruction.

'Find me something I can put down his throat that will grip. Try the jewellery stall.'

Kirby heard Nick's mellow voice instructing Jade as she counted and puffed five breaths into the unconscious man.

The moment she raised her head, Nick applied the same pressure again over Gaz's ribs, thrusting downward and forward.

Kirby rechecked Gaz's airway, hoping to feel the firm fruit.

Her stomach rolled. 'Still nothing.' She gave Gaz another five breaths, panic starting to ripple through her. If they couldn't secure his airway soon, he'd go into cardiac arrest.

'I've got these.' Jade came running back and handed Nick a pair of long, thin pliers.

Kirby's fingers detected a faint beat. 'Pulse, weak and thready. He's going to need an emergency tracheostomy to bypass the blockage and avoid arresting. Jenny, pass me the scalpel blade.'

'Hang on a mo.' Nick spoke quietly but decisively. 'Give me half a minute with these sort of forceps and see if I grab the strawberry.'

Kirby didn't want to waste any more precious time. 'But we don't have a laryngoscope for you to visualise the trachea.'

Green eyes flashed with ready understanding. 'I've done it before in EMD.'

A blurry image played at the edge of her mind but immediately faded, overtaken by her focus on the emergency. 'What do you need me to do?'

'Steady his head for me.'

'Will do.' His confidence reassured her and she placed her hands over her patient's ears, two fingers still resting on his carotid pulse.

The scream of the ambulance's siren broke over the tense crowd, the sound both urgent and comforting as it brought the medical equipment they really needed.

'Here goes.' Nick shot her a look that said, *Nothing ventured, nothing gained*, and lowered the thin, silver pliers into the slack throat of the unconscious man. 'Can't feel anything, damn it.' His long fingers carefully controlled all the minute movements with stunning expertise.

Kirby kept her gaze on Nick's hand, willing it to find the obstruction. Time spiralled out, each second an agonising wait. Garry's pulse suddenly faltered under her fingers. 'No pulse. Get out now. I'm starting CPR.'

Nick immediately pulled his left arm back, and a soft, half-dissolved strawberry hung limply from the tip of the forceps. 'Got it. Roll him over.'

Kirby moved her patient's head to the side as he started coughing violently and vomited up a stream of pale pink liquid onto the ground.

Relief surged through her as she checked his pulse. 'Pulse back, patient breathing.' She looked up into Nick's face, as the worry lines on the bridge of his nose faded. She experienced a sense of déjà vu. 'Lucky save.'

He nodded, a slow smile appearing through the stubble on his jaw. 'Very lucky.'

'Kirby!'

She turned to see Theo and Richard, the ambulance officers, running toward her. 'Great timing, guys. We need all your gear.' She grabbed the black oxygen cylinder with its distinctive white top and quickly unravelled the pale green tubing. Gently, she lifted Garry's head and looped the elastic over his ears, adjusting the Hudson mask. 'This will help you breathe.'

The sick and bewildered man gripped her arm. 'Thanks, Doc.' His voice rasped out the words. 'I couldn't breathe… It scared the hell out of me…worse than being on the boat in a storm.'

She smiled down at him. 'I'm glad I was here, but really it was Dr…' She realised she didn't know his surname. 'Nick? I didn't catch your surname.'

He finished attaching the Lifepak electrodes and scanned the ECG tracing before looking up and speaking straight to Garry. 'I'm Dr Nick Dennison, and I'm just glad I was two stalls over.'

Nick Dennison. Kirby did a double-take so fast she almost cricked her neck, the name having instant recognition in her brain. But the man in front of her looked nothing like how she remembered Melbourne City Hospital's up-and-coming emergency care specialist. What on earth was he doing in Port Bathurst, selling organic fruit and vegetables?

CHAPTER TWO

NICK concentrated hard, keeping his gaze firmly on the cannula he was inserting into Garry's arm, immensely glad of the distraction. Kirby Atherton's sky-blue eyes sparkled hypnotically, like light dancing on water. It had been the first thing he'd noticed about her when she'd walked up to his stall, quickly followed by her willowy height and the way her running gear clung deliciously to every feminine curve.

But it had been her eyes that had really drawn him. He had the craziest sensation that if her eyes were deep pools of water and he dived into them, he would emerge changed somehow. He tried to shrug the irrational feeling away. Not even on his worst days last year, when he'd hardly been able to get out of bed and the drugs he'd been taking had made him despair, had he experienced such foolish thoughts.

And prior to being sick, when life had consisted of work and a revolving door of beautiful women, he'd *never* thought twice about a set of eyes. Perhaps his mother was right. Maybe he had been out of social circulation for too long.

Brushing away the unsettling thoughts, he released the tourniquet, watching the flow of saline, checking for problems, and refocusing on far more straightforward things. 'We're going start you on antibiotics, Garry.'

The exhausted patient just nodded from behind his mask.

The two burly paramedics lowered their stretcher in preparation to transfer Garry from the ground to the slightly more comfortable but narrow gurney.

'Do you need a hand?' Nick taped the drip firmly in place.

'We'll be right, thanks, Doc. We do this all the time so we're in the swing. Best help you can give us is to just step back out of the way.' Theo locked the brakes of the stretcher with his foot.

He stood up and moved to the side at the same moment as Kirby. Much of her fine blonde hair had escaped its pink elastic hair tie and strands blew across her flushed cheeks. Her scent tantalised his nostrils, a blend of exercise and glowing health overlaid with a swirl of flowers and berries. He breathed in deeply.

'I'm going to ring through to Barago Hospital.'

Her words brought him back to the task at hand and he caught her sideways glance—the look quick but questioningly intense—as if she thought she should consult with him.

Her mouth opened ready to speak and then her teeth suddenly dragged across her bottom lip, momentarily flattening it before the skin rebounded into shape—full, soft and rose red.

Blood pounded through his veins with an unexpected rush and it took every ounce of concentration to stay connected to the conversation. Hell, what was wrong with him? Had he stepped back so far from his previous life that he'd disconnected from things and lost the ability to focus? He ran his hand though his short hair, missing the satisfaction of being able to tug at its length. Once he'd been known for his single-mindedness and right now he wanted that back.

She spoke again, this time her words less certain. 'I think he should be evacuated and have a bronchoscopy.'

She reminded him of a resident who knew her stuff but lacked confidence in her judgement. It was a scenario he was used to but today it surprised him because as a country GP she must be used to making decisions all the time. Glad to be back on familiar territory, he moved to reassure her.

'It's a good call. The choking might have been an accident but he's at an age where you need to rule out multiple sclerosis or other muscular conditions.'

'Let's hope it was just an accident, Nick *Dennison*.' She raised light brown brows at him. 'You are *the* Nick Dennison, youngest appointed head of Emergency Medicine in Australia?'

He studied her pretty features, looking for something that would spark his memory, but nothing did. Surely if they'd dated or worked together he would never have forgotten those eyes. He shoved his hands in his pockets, knowing there was no point denying the truth. 'That's me. I'm sorry, have we met before?'

She shook her head. 'Not really. I attended one of your lectures when I was a resident at Prince William Hospital. I was on duty that night and wasn't able to go to the dinner afterwards, but I think you met a friend of mine, Virginia Charters.' She shot him a knowing look. One that said, *You didn't call.*

He had no recollection of Virginia Charters but then again, that entire lecture tour had been a blur of cities, lecture theatres and women eager to date him. He loved women and he loved dating. He just didn't love or date one woman.

He took a punt on the type of women he'd accepted invitations from, women he'd wined, dined and satisfied before his world had imploded. Before he'd lost complete interest. 'Ah, Virginia…brunette and vivacious?'

He caught the surprised and almost disappointed look cross her face that he sounded like he'd remembered.

'Yes, that's Virginia. I'm sorry I didn't recognise you but you look very different from how I remember.'

He grinned, wanting to keep things light. He had no intention of telling her what had happened to him. He had no intention of anyone in Port ever knowing. His time here was all about wellness and no way was he looking back. 'It's the lack of a suit, a lectern and the slide presentation glowing behind me.'

Her mouth immediately widened into a broad smile that soared to her amazing eyes. Eyes that filled with coloured prisms, the many hues of blue which spun and twirled like the shards in a kaleidoscope.

His heart jolted hard in his chest and his breath stalled as a flicker of almost forgotten heat surged deep inside him.

Lust?

Yes! He wanted to whoop with delight.

His libido had vanished the day his world had changed but today it was back, albeit dusty and creaky. Four months of opting out of the mainstream and concentrating on his health was paying off. His body was back.

Suddenly his fascination with her eyes, her mouth and her curves made sense. It wasn't Kirby Atherton per se. She just happened to be the first pretty woman he'd come across that coincided with his recovery. He relaxed into the knowledge as his world came reassuringly back into kilter.

Kirby briskly went through the motions of handing over Garry's care to the Barago Hospital and organising Jake into the care of his aunt. Four phone calls and an hour later she had it all sorted but throughout the process her mind had buzzed continuously with the fact that Melbourne's most well-known ER doctor, the man aptly dubbed 'the playboy doctor', was in sleepy Port Bathurst.

The stories about him said he worked hard and played hard and he was well known for hitting the trendy clubs and bars until the early hours. He and her friend Virginia had shared an intense twenty-four hours and Kirby had been the shoulder Virginia had cried on when he hadn't called afterwards. She'd also been the voice of reason, pointing out that Ginny had virtually thrown herself at him and to give the man credit, he'd never promised her anything other than a good time. That he'd apparently delivered.

At the time, Kirby had had the advantage of distance because she had been cheerfully engaged, blissfully happy and busy planning her future of marriage, motherhood and medicine. Although she could appreciate the model good looks of urbane and sophisticated men like Nick, she'd always fallen for the guy-next-door type—the home-town handyman slash family man.

Anthony only talked about fixing things, remember? Then he hired someone else to do it.

She shoved away the unwanted thought that reminded her of how blind she'd been and refocussed on the memories of her friend. Ginny had been the one to go for tall dark and handsome. Except Nick hadn't been dark then, he'd been blond, which was part of the reason she hadn't recognised him. Today his hair was shorter and darker and physically he was thinner but more toned.

She ran her fingers through her hair. Nick Dennison and Port Bathurst just didn't match. Port didn't have a cutting-edge emergency department and as for nightlife, well, the recent crazy whist night at the tennis club had pushed the envelope. Lasting until midnight, the hall had rocked because someone had brought along their CD player and got people up to dance after the cards had finished. Nick in Port was like the translated instruction booklet that came with her new bookshelves—it made no sense. Her mind went round and round, stuck in a loop.

Who cares why he's here? He's a doctor with a wealth of experience.

The truth sliced sharply through everything else, stripping away all irrelevancies. Nick was a doctor and she needed a doctor *and* a mentor. The equation balanced perfectly. Nick working in Port alongside her meant she could stay in the town.

It didn't matter that he was a party boy, a smooth-as-silk charmer and heart-stoppingly gorgeous. She'd given up men and men like Nick had never been her type anyway. No, this would be a professional association only and keep her GP training on schedule.

The only thing left to do was ask him if he would work the summer season with her. Rolling back her shoulders, she headed toward the market to professionally proposition Dr Nick Dennison.

She arrived at Nick's stall and her heart skipped a beat as she watched him in complete control but cloaked by a lazy charm. Out of his suit and white coat he looked much more like the sort of guy she'd once been attracted to. *Breathe. This one is not for you. No man is for you.*

He was serving a customer, his amazing green eyes and his total attention completely focussed on Phyllis Gutherson, Port's resident naysayer. But her usually sour expression had vanished and in its place was a girlish smile. She looked twenty years younger.

Waiting her turn and shaking her head in wonder at how he'd achieved such a miracle, Kirby bobbed down next to Nick's dog and scratched his ears. 'Your master could charm diamonds from jewel thieves, couldn't he?'

Large brown eyes gazed adoringly up at her as the dog laid his head in her lap.

'Turbo, stop it.'

At the sound of the deep, commanding voice, both the dog and Kirby looked up.

A smile met her gaze. A smile that fizzed intoxicatingly through her like the bubbles of champagne. Her bent knees liquefied and she wobbled slightly as she rose to her feet.

He leaned casually against the stall table. 'That dog will turn on the charm if he thinks it will get him something.'

'Gosh, and I wonder where he learned that from.' She shook her head, laughing. 'You just managed to make Port Bathurst history by getting Phyllis Gutherson to smile, and charming her into buying your last item of produce. I mean, who eats radishes?'

This time his grin had a tinge of guilt to it, not dissimilar to that of a kid caught out sneaking biscuits too close to dinner. 'I will concede I might have used a well-placed compliment or two to move the radishes but, hey, I just sold everything I harvested for my first market.' He raised his hand as his eyes danced with elation—joy, pure and simple.

Without thought, she raised her hand to meet his, drawn completely by his enthusiastic aura that seemed to wrap around her, pulling her in. Her palm connected with his in a slap of celebration.

Heat tore through her hard and fast, ricocheting from skin to muscle to deep tissue and fanning out until every cell vibrated with its legacy and she tingled all over. Tingled in a way she never had before, not even with Anthony, the man she'd loved and thought she'd be spending the rest of her life with. Horrified, she jerked her arm back to the safety of her side.

Remember why you're here. She swallowed hard and cleared her throat. 'That's fabulous. Congratulations. Can I buy you a cup of coffee to help you celebrate and to say thank you for your help with Garry?'

'Thanks for the offer, but I have to pack up here first and I don't want to hold you up.' He picked up some boxes and stowed them into the back of a ute.

Kirby hauled her gaze away from his rippling biceps and tried to keep her focus on why she was actually here. She didn't just want to blurt out, 'Please work with me.' The situation needed more finesse than that. 'How about I give you a hand and then we go for coffee?' *Don't sound so needy.* 'If that suits you.'

Emerald eyes studied her for a brief moment. 'OK, it's a deal.' He tipped over the wooden trestle and grabbed the old metal supports, his broad palm wrapping deftly around them.

Kirby had a sudden image of a leather tool belt sitting flat across his washboard abdomen and him fixing all her sticking sash windows. *Stay focussed. He's a doctor, not a handyman.*

'Excellent.' She passed him boxes and watched him stack them as if they were a mathematical problem. 'How long have you been in Port?'

'Technically, I'm not in Port because I don't live here.' He slid the long trestle into the ute.

Kirby's gut went into freefall. With his vegetable selling

she'd assumed he lived here. Her plan depended on him living close by.

He paused in his stacking and extended a muscular arm out toward the mountainous rainforest area behind the town. 'My property's Riversleigh, thirty K out, near Sheep-wash Corner.'

Her gut steadied. She was still in the game—just. Sheep-wash Corner was pretty isolated, even more out of the way than Port. Nick Dennison hadn't just left Melbourne for Sleepy Hollow, he'd gone bush, a tree-change. But why? The situation got even more intriguing. 'How long have you lived out there?'

His cheerful open face suddenly closed, and the dimples in his cheeks smoothed over. 'Four months.'

He handed her one end of a tarpaulin. 'What about you?'

She caught the deft change, the power switch in the conversation, and she pulled the tarp tight, just like her mother had taught her as a child when she folded sheets. He didn't want to talk about why he was here. 'I've been here since the start of the month.' She walked up to him to match her corners to his.

'Is this a long-term plan for you?' His fingers slid over hers as he moved to accept the tarp.

The sharp tingle of sensation almost made her drop her corners and she found herself gripping them instead of releasing them into his hands. The moment she let go, she flexed her fingers, willing the shimmering away.

Since the age of twelve Kirby had been tall and she was used to being a similar height to many men. But she had to tilt her head to look up into Nick's face. It disconcerted her. *He* disconcerted her. 'It's a summer plan to start with. I'm doing a six-month GP rotation.' *Six months to pull herself together.*

'A summer by the sea. Sounds relaxing.' His dimples reappeared, deepening as he smiled.

Her heartbeat seemed to skip. How could one man's smile make her feel almost dizzy? *This is your opening—grab it.* The practical words broke into the haze that enveloped her brain. 'Actually, apart from a run along the pier in the mornings, that is as close as I've got to the beach.'

He slapped his palm down on the tailgate of the ute and Turbo immediately jumped onto the tray, turned around and lay down. 'Quiet Port Bathurst been keeping you busy?'

'It's hardly quiet! Between the residents, the work with Kids' Cottage and now the tourists arriving, I can barely get to the laundrette on a Sunday to do my washing. I had easier days back at Royal William.' She stared straight up at him. 'I'm surprised the hospital board didn't approach you when you moved down here.'

His hands stilled for a fraction on the tailgate. 'Until this morning, the hospital board didn't know I was a doctor.' He slammed the back of the ute shut and wiped his hands on an old towel. 'No one did.'

His words stunned her. 'Why on earth not?'

A shadow passed through his eyes, like a cloud scudding across the sun. 'Because I didn't come here to practise medicine.'

Her plan, so clear and perfect in her head, took a massive broadside hit, but she wasn't letting go just yet. 'But you're a talented doctor and Port needs you.'

Dark brows drew together, causing a crease at the bridge of his nose. 'No, it doesn't, Kirby. Port's got you. Besides, I'm an accident and emergency specialist, not a GP, and right now I'm really not interested in working.'

She wanted to stamp her feet. She had the ideal mentor in front of her and he didn't want to work. She chewed her lip as her limited options ran through her head. With a deep breath she played the only card she had left in her deck.

Honesty. She raised her gaze to his and spoke from the heart. 'Without your help, I can't work here.'

Over the last couple of months Nick had said an enthusiastic 'No' to five job offers from hospitals around the country with barely a second thought about his decision. But one glance from Kirby's blue eyes, swirling with honesty and tinged with pleading, and suddenly every reason for not working was teetering on unsteady foundations. 'What do you mean, you can't work here without my help?'

'How well do you know Port?'

'I don't really know it at all. I come here for the market but I use Barago as my centre for supplies as it's bigger.'

She laced her fingers, moving them back and forth against the backs of her hands. 'Soon after I arrived in Port, Christopher Grayson, the town's GP, fell ill.'

Ignoring the wavering feeling, he stuck firmly to the facts. 'When is Grayson due back?'

Her gaze held his with a steady look. 'He's not. Unfortunately, he had a stroke and he's currently in rehab.'

He shoved his hands in his pockets, empathy weaving through him for a man who had a battle on his hands. But this wasn't his problem and there was another solution. The foundations steadied. 'So you advertise for another doctor to help you with the workload.'

She sighed, tucking stray hair behind her ear. 'It's not just the workload. I came to Port as part of my GP rotation.'

The image of her tugging at her bottom lip when she was deciding to send Garry to Barago beamed against his brain. His chest tightened. Suddenly her hesitancy and lack of confidence made sense. 'Please don't tell me this is your first six-month GP rotation.'

'It is.'

Damn it. He slammed his right fist into his left hand. 'So without supervision you can't practise?' But the question was rhetorical, he knew the answer.

'Not in Port, no.'

He wasn't ready to work in medicine just yet. He'd promised himself six more months, just savouring being well. Hell, surely he deserved that after everything he'd been through. He ran his hand across the back of his neck, trying to sort out his thoughts. He had no connection with this woman, no reason to turn his plans upside down to help her. The obvious solution shot into his head. 'You could go elsewhere to do your rotation or back to Royal William.'

A shudder of tension moved through her. 'Royal William isn't an option I want to pursue. Look, Port has already lost one doctor, so it can't afford to lose me.' She tilted her head and the brilliant blue of her eyes flickered over him, pulling hard at his sense of duty. 'And you wouldn't do that to a rural community who's so enthusiastically embraced your organic vegetable venture, would you?'

The words hit like a flyball, hard and unexpected. The woman in front of him with her long, blonde hair, honey-gold skin and an air of vulnerability had suddenly transformed from a pleading porcelain doll to a steely blackmailer. He could turn down large hospitals where there were plenty of other contenders for the job but she had him backed into a corner where his 'no' would impact on many hard-working people.

He wanted to kick the tyres on the ute, he wanted to be back on the farm digging over beds filled with fragrant soil, he wanted to be anywhere but here, dealing with an unwinnable ethical dilemma. He crossed his arms and took in a deep breath. 'That's true, no town deserves to be without a doctor.'

'So you will work in Port this summer?' Expectation and enthusiastic anticipation filled her voice.

A flood of heat collided with frustration. Well, she wasn't getting everything her own way. 'I'll mentor you and give you the supervision you need, but I'm warning you now, I'm a tough teacher and I'll expect one hundred and ten per cent.' The words came out on a growl—the one he'd perfected to keep his interns on their toes. 'But as for working, well, it will be with *strict* conditions.'

He waited, expecting to see signs of anxiety at his mild threat about being a tough teacher, and he certainly expected to see both disappointment and hear questions about the conditions he planned to impose.

But her mouth widened into a smile that raced to her eyes and seemed to dance around her like the white light of sparklers. 'That's fantastic. You won't regret this, Nick, it will be a fabulous summer.'

But every single part of him regretted it already.

CHAPTER THREE

KIRBY sat and stirred her coffee at an outside table, looking down and watching the white foam of her latte blend into the hot milk. Nick sat opposite her. Usually she chose this table so she could admire the view of the bay and enjoy gazing at the pelicans, fascinated by the way they lowered their feet in preparation for a water landing.

But today she'd caught herself admiring the way Nick's thick brown eyelashes almost touched his cheeks when he blinked and how the new streaks of silver against his temples gave him a look of authority. Unwanted tendrils of attraction had tightened inside her and she'd glanced away. It was a lot safer to stare at her coffee.

Nick moved the straw of his smoothie up and down through the dense blend of fresh fruits. Apparently he didn't drink coffee. This was yet another surprise as every doctor she knew considered coffee a vital part of their day, but absolutely nothing about this man fitted the picture of the doctor she'd expected. However, despite everything being at odds with expectation, he'd offered to help her and that was all that mattered.

'You're missing out on an amazing flavour just for a superficial caffeine buzz.' He winked at her as he drank his fruit concoction, his Adam's apple moving rhythmically and hypnotically against his taut muscular neck.

A rush of heat burned her cheeks and she dragged her eyes away. 'It's not just the buzz, it's the flavour of hazelnut.' She already had a buzz and she hadn't even taken a sip of her coffee. It had started simmering inside her from the moment he'd said he would mentor her. It felt oddly strange and yet deliciously wonderful and she was pretty sure it was relief.

You can call it relief if you want to.

She immediately took an indignant sip of her coffee and turned a deaf ear to the voice inside her head. Of course it was relief. Her search for a doctor was over and now she could stay in Port for her full six months. *Stay a long way from Anthony and Lisa.*

'Tell me about the demographics of Port Bathurst.' Nick pushed his large shake container off to the side, his eyes fixed firmly on her and filled with businesslike intent.

Kirby relaxed under his professional gaze. This was the working relationship she'd anticipated when she'd asked him to mentor her. 'Fishing and farming are the main industries but life is tough in both. Many young people are leaving town, although the mayor was telling me that recently there's been a push to increase tourism. A new diving business has opened in the main street, along with charter fishing trips, "Surf the wave" classes and catered cycling holidays.'

He nodded. 'I sold vegetables from the farm gate to a family on a Gypsy Caravan adventure the other week. They'd started out from Port and were taking the back roads. Regeneration is really important for rural communities like this.' He leaned back in his chair. 'So, how does all of this impact on the medical services?'

'It keeps us busy. The clinic is attached to the hospital and there are six acute beds and a small emergency centre plus midwifery. Major traumas get airlifted to Melbourne after being stabilised here and elective surgery goes to Barago. We have a large elderly population and the hospital has a nursing-home wing which is currently full. Oh, and then there's Kids' Cottage.'

His eyes darkened slightly. 'What's that?'

She leaned forward as her enthusiasm for KC spilled out. 'It's a fabulous holiday camp for children. They have camps for sick children with chronic illnesses, they have camps for healthy kids who have siblings with chronic illnesses or disabilities, and they have camps for kids whose families are struggling emotionally or financially and just need a bit of breathing space.'

Nick's fingers started to unroll the rim of the shake container. 'But Kids' Cottage would have their own medical staff, right?'

She shook her head. 'No, the town has always provided medical assistance since it started one hundred years ago. It's something that the locals are very proud of.'

A muscle twitched in his jaw. 'That's one of my conditions.'

Laughter bubbled up inside her. 'Are you going to fight me for first dibs on working with the kids?' A nurturing warmth filled her, tinged with regret. 'But I know what you mean, the cottage was a big drawcard for me to come to Port.'

His mouth firmed into an uncompromising line. 'There'll be no fight. I don't want to work at the camp so you can happily keep all that work for yourself.'

She blinked, completely startled. 'But the camp is so much fun. Why on earth don't you want to work there?'

The waxy cardboard unravelled in his hands, pulled apart by rigid fingers. 'I said I'd help you but there'd be conditions. This is one of them.'

His usually mellow voice was suddenly brusque and for the first time she caught a glimpse of the 'doctor in charge', the doctor used to issuing orders and being instantly obeyed without question. It caught her by surprise and a jolt of anger speared her. She tilted her chin—she wasn't a green first-year resident. 'What do you have against working with children?'

A streak of something she couldn't really define flared in his eyes for the briefest moment, before being cloaked by a spark of irritation. 'I didn't say I had anything against working with children, I'm just exerting my right not to.'

His arrogance astounded her. 'I suppose you had a paediatric registrar to save you from such work.'

'That's right.'

The blunt words hit her, their uncompromising tone harsh and decisive. 'Well, there's no paediatric registrar in Port so what about children who come into the clinic?'

His mouth flattened into an obdurate line. 'On the unlikely chance you're not available, I'll see them.'

'Well, that's reassuring.' The sarcastic words leapt off her lips as a fizz of frustration spread through her. 'Do you have any other demographic groups you refuse to work with? Any other conditions I should know about before we start?'

His eyebrows rose in a perfect arch at her mockery, but when he spoke his tone was all steely business. 'This is how I see it working. Each weekday morning I'll meet you at seven a.m. for the nursing-home ward round and I'll work half-day clinics Monday to Friday with lunchtime case-review sessions as part of your supervision. I'll be unavailable on Saturdays because I'll be at the market.' He extended his arm toward her, every part of him vibrating with tension. 'Deal or no deal?'

She recognised the adversarial glint in his eyes as a

thousand questions hammered in her head and poured into her mouth, demanding instant answers. She couldn't understand why he wouldn't work at the camp. Why he would prefer not to see the children at the clinic—none of it made sense, but she swallowed hard against every single question, forcing them down deep. If she quizzed him too closely on why he wouldn't work at KC he would walk, and she couldn't risk that. He had her well and truly cornered and she had no choice.

Slowly, she stretched out her right hand and slid her smaller palm against his. Work-hardened calluses scraped gently over her softer skin in a tantalising caress as his fingers wrapped around her hand. His heat poured through her, racing along her arm, radiating into her chest, tightening her breasts and then burrowing down deep inside until every part of her had liquefied with desire. Yet a dangerous vixen-voice betrayed her, demanding even more.

No, no, I'm not doing this. I am immune to men. But her body disagreed. His touch was unlike any handshake she'd ever known and she breathed in sharply, trying to grasp control of her wayward and wanton body which longed to drape itself over the chair and purr with pleasure. She finally found her own voice and hoped it sounded firm and business-like. 'Deal.'

A smile roved across his face, creating twinkling dimples in his cheeks, sparking emerald lights in his eyes and completely eliminating all signs of his previous tension. 'Deal it is, then.'

'Wonderful.' The word came out horrifyingly breathy, the vixen having gained control. Suddenly the deal that would keep her in Port, well away from Anthony and her shattered dreams, was no longer the 'get-out-of-jail-free card' that she'd expected.

* * *

'But, Doctor, are you sure you've seen enough?' Mrs Norton's rheumy blue eyes sparkled as arthritic fingers fumbled over the pearl buttons on her crocheted bedjacket.

'Let me help you with that.' Nick smiled as he quickly buttoned the jacket on the elderly woman who would have been a stunning beauty in her younger days. 'If you can flirt with me, Mrs N. then you're doing just fine, but I have adjusted the diuretic so that should make breathing a little easier.'

'Thank you, Doctor.' She touched his hand as he finished latching the last button. 'And when will you be in to see me next, dear?'

'Tomorrow morning.'

'I'll be ready.' She gave him a wave as he left the room.

Mrs Norton was the last nursing-home patient on his morning round's list and over the last hour he'd met all the residents. Every female patient had held his hand and flirted with him as well as showing him pictures of their granddaughters and great-granddaughters. *'She's a wonderful cook, Doctor, and you could do with some fattening up.'* The male patients had gruffly given him fishing tips, shaken their heads at his choice of football team and told him the 'sure-fire' solution to aphids—*'garlic and soapy water, Doc.'*

After working in emergency medicine for years, he'd expected to find a nursing-home round slow and boring work. He didn't know if it was because he hadn't worked in almost two years and today he was just enjoying being back in the field, but he'd been surprised at how much fun he'd had chatting with them all. The moment he got home he was going to make up that aphid-fighting mixture and use it on his tomatoes this afternoon.

He glanced at his phone and read a text from Kirby asking

him to meet her at the clinic. She hadn't made it to rounds, having been called out at six a.m. to Kids' Cottage.

He'd had no idea the town had a kids' holiday camp dating back a hundred years. When he'd initially said he would have conditions attached to working here, he'd been thinking about how he would juggle the farm with practising medicine and still have precious time for himself. He hadn't realised he would need to use the 'conditions' banner for anything else, but no way was he going to be the medico for a kids' camp.

He shuddered as the memory of his father's voice suddenly sounded in his head. *You have to go, mate. You'll enjoy it if you give it a chance.*

He'd hated the enforced time he'd spent at camps as a kid and he sure as hell wasn't spending time there as an adult. This time he had a choice and he was choosing to say no.

Suddenly the vision of Kirby's wide blue eyes aimed squarely at him and full of disapproval shoved his father's voice out of his head. Damn it, *he* was the experienced doctor and he had the right to say where he would work without giving a full-on explanation. He was so *not* revisiting his childhood, especially not with a woman whose eyes threatened to see down to his soul.

Better that she thought him a jerk than to go there.

Yeah, right. You go ahead and think that if it makes you feel better.

He ran his hand across his hair, short spikes meeting his palm, and he grunted in frustration. Hell, he didn't even have to be working in Port! This time here was supposed to be all about wellness and focussing on himself. He was the one doing *her* the favour.

Shaking his head to clear it of unwanted images, errant

thoughts and the eminently reasonable voice of his father, he strode toward the clinic, which was attached to the small emergency department of Port Bathurst Bush Nursing Hospital. Pushing open the door, which was covered in healthy-lifestyle posters, he stepped into the waiting room.

'Good morning. You must be Dr Dennison. Welcome!' A woman who looked to be in her early fifties with spiked, short red hair walked toward him, extending her hand. 'I'm Meryl Jeffries, the practice nurse, and it's wonderful that you're here.' She pumped his hand firmly and didn't draw breath. 'The whole town is talking about how you used Cheryl's jewellery pliers to pull that strawberry out of Garry's throat, and thank goodness you were there. Anyway, Kirby is just giving Theo the scoop on young Harrison, who thought that he'd start the day by jumping off the top bunk and fracturing his tib and fib so she'll be here in a minute and, well, here she is now so I'll let her give you the tour as I've got my baby clinic.' She threw her arm out behind her toward the reception desk. 'But if you need anything just ask because Vicki and I have been here for years.'

Vicki, who looked a bit older than Meryl, glanced up from the computer and smiled at him over the top of her bright purple glasses. 'Lovely to have you here, Dr D., and, like Meryl said, just yell. My only rule is that you bring the histories back to me as you greet your next patient so they can be filed or else things get lost. Oh, and I made you a ginger fluff sponge and it's in the kitchen so help yourself to as much as you like because you do look a bit on the thin side, dear.'

He opened his mouth but words escaped him. It was like work had just collided with his mother—instructions and praise all rolled into one with a slightly disapproving look thrown in. 'Ah, thank you for the welcome and the cake.'

They both nodded and smiled and then Vicki returned to her computer screen and Meryl disappeared down the corridor.

'I see you've met Meryl and Vicki.' A familiar tinkling laugh sounded behind him.

He turned around to find a smiling Kirby walking toward him. Her hair moved in sync with her body, brushing across her shoulders and floating around her face. On Saturday she'd been wearing Lycra running gear. Today she wore a summer dress with a close-fitting scoop-neck top that hugged her waist before opening out into a short full skirt that showcased her shapely long, tanned legs. Bright red painted nails peeked out of strappy sandals.

Heat poured through him and zeroed in on his groin, making him dizzy. His reaction to her was so much stronger than two days ago and that made no sense at all. On Saturday she'd had a bare midriff and figure-hugging clothes on so of course his body had reacted. Hell, he'd been pleased it had because it meant things were finally getting back to normal despite the fact he'd always preferred brunettes.

But today far more clothes covered Kirby's body and yet the hidden curves tantalised even more. He dragged his gaze up from the hint of creamy breast back to her face and prayed she hadn't noticed his lapse of professionalism. He might have been known for dating many women but he'd *always* kept work and pleasure distinctly separate. He never dated someone he worked with directly so he definitely needed to get back into the work saddle again if those lines were blurring.

He rubbed his jaw. 'Those two are like a hurricane. Are they always like that?'

'Always.' A more serious expression played around her mouth. 'But don't be deceived—they really know their stuff and the clinic runs like clockwork. Vicki's children are adults and living in Melbourne now so I think she's missing mothering and she's making up for it with us.' Her eyes danced, softening the indignant look that streaked across her face. 'Although I've *never* had a cake made for me.'

He answered without thinking. 'You can have as much as you like. I really don't eat cakes.'

'First no coffee and now no cake?' She tilted her head enquiringly, a glint of interrogation in her eyes. 'Next you'll be telling me you don't drink.'

He smiled, falling back into old habits in an attempt to deflect her. 'I do drink but only top-shelf wine on special occasions.' He didn't really want to talk about why he'd given up cakes and cream. 'So how about you show me around the clinic and the emergency department of the hospital and then I can get started.'

Work. After all, that was why he was here. He itched to throw himself into a busy day because working seemed a heck of a lot safer than talking about himself or ogling a colleague's décolletage.

'Can I run something past you?' Kirby caught Nick between patients.

'Sure. What's up?' His eyes darkened to the colour of moss as he swung around on the office chair, his gaze fixed firmly on her.

A gaze so intense that her skin tingled. *Get over yourself. You asked the man a question and he's giving you his undivided attention, just as a colleague should.* She gripped

Melinda Nikoloski's history and focussed on the facts. 'I've got a thirty-five-year-old woman with general fatigue, enlarged glands, persistent cough, raspy voice and episodes of shortness of breath.'

'On bare facts alone it sounds like summer flu.' His mouth tweaked up on the left in a thoughtful smile. 'But you wouldn't be running it past me if you thought it was flu.'

She slid into the chair next to his desk, grateful for his intuition. Grateful that he was here. Leaping into this job a year before most people started a GP rotation had stretched her, but she'd been desperate to leave Melbourne, desperate to distance herself from everything that reminded her of what she'd lost, and Port had been desperate enough to accept her. 'The previous doctor saw her a month ago, made a diagnosis of flu and prescribed bronchodilators for the shortness of breath.'

He tapped his silver pen on a notepad. 'So how is she now?'

'Not much better.' Kirby chewed her bottom lip in thought. 'She could be anaemic, like many women in their mid-thirties are, so on Friday I ordered a routine full blood examination and those results should be back shortly, but even so, I have a nagging feeling about it. Totally non-scientific, I know, but nagging none the less.'

Understanding lined his face. 'Listening to your gut feeling is an important part of being a good doctor. Out here you don't have access to the full weight of diagnostic tests that you get in a large hospital.'

He sat forward, his hands flat on the spun cotton of his summer trousers which so casually covered what she imagined to be solid, muscular thighs. 'A persistent cough and shortness of breath can too easily be attributed to asthma. As we've got an X-ray machine, let's do a chest X-ray. It's a simple test and hopefully we can rule out a lung mass.'

'But she's not a smoker and has no other risk factors.'

He shrugged. 'There are *other* masses that can be found in the chest. But that said, it's important to remember that non-smoking females are dying from lung cancer because it's being missed in the early stages of the disease. Granted, the air down here is cleaner than other places but you don't know what she's been exposed to.' He tugged on the hair just behind his ear, his voice rising slightly. 'Hell, we don't know half of what we're exposed to in the air or in our food.'

His heartfelt reaction surprised her. He sounded more like an environmentalist than a doctor. But, then again, he did grow organic vegetables and he didn't drink coffee. Two things she knew he hadn't done two years ago because Virginia had basically told her everything about this citified man who'd loved the good things in life. 'OK, I'll organise a chest X-ray. Thanks.'

'No problem, it's what I'm here for.' He spun back on his chair, his attention returning to the article he'd been reading when she'd walked into the room.

Familiar disappointment slugged her and she tried to shrug it off because there was *no* reason to feel like this. Nick had done his job well. Very well. *He's the mentor, you're the student. That's what you want and that's what you're getting.*

She continued to remind herself of that against the strange hollow feeling in her gut as she walked back to her consulting room. Glad of something to do, she picked up the phone and called Melinda, asking her to come in for a chest X-ray.

Melinda sat in the chair, her face pale with black smudges under her eyes. She rubbed her knee. 'I think I should have got an X-ray of my knee as well as my chest. It's been sore for the last week.' She sighed. 'I really hope the chest X-ray will tell you what's wrong with me because I'm sick of feeling like this and I think I'm getting worse, not better.'

Kirby silently agreed with her patient—Melinda had the pasty pallor of someone extremely unwell. She slid the black and white film onto the light box and flicked on the light. Using her pen she outlined the image. 'Your heart is here and it's the normal size, and if there was any fluid on your lungs or infection that would show up as white on the film. But your lungs are pretty clear, which is why they look black.' *And you don't have a tumour, thank goodness.*

'But I feel so awful.' Tears welled up in the woman's eyes. 'I'm so grumpy, the kids and Dev are avoiding me and all I want to do is sleep but I keep going hot and cold and my joints ache.'

'Just hot at night?' Piece by piece she tried to match up the vague symptoms. She rechecked the X-ray but there was no lower lobe consolidation, no sign of pneumonia.

Melinda wrung her hands. 'Sometimes during the day too.'

'Are you still menstruating?' Menopause was unlikely but Kirby had learned the hard way that sometimes the unexpected happened.

Her patient grimaced. 'Oh, yes, I'm doing that too well—flooding, in fact.'

Which led Kirby back to her initial thoughts from Friday. Menstruating women were often anaemic—lacking in iron could make you feel pretty low. *But not give you hot flushes.* The words nagged at Kirby. Perhaps she needed to run a test for hormone levels and do blood cultures as well.

She glanced at her watch and picked up the phone to speak to Vicki. 'The courier should have arrived with the results of your blood test and hopefully the results will say I need to prescribe you my famous orange-juice-and-parsley iron-boosting drink.

'If that's the case, in two weeks you'll feel like a new woman and we can discuss your options to reduce your menstrual bleeding.' She smiled, trying to reassure her patient despite an enveloping sense of gloom that Melinda's condition would not be that simple and neither would it have such a straightforward solution.

But she *had* to be wrong. Right now she didn't trust her gut at all, given the way her body melted into a mush of pulsating need at one smile from Nick. How could one smile from a man she knew to be a womanising charmer undermine everything she'd learned at the hands of Anthony? *Face it, Kirby*, he'd said. *You can't give me what I need.*

She knew better than to get involved again—this time she knew in advance what the outcome would be and she wasn't putting her hand or heart up for another brutal and soul-destroying rejection. No, now she was a lot wiser and she knew better than to let attraction blind her to a handsome man. But her body wasn't listening to her brain and it betrayed her every time she clapped eyes on Nick. No, she definitely didn't trust her gut, because right now her radar was really out of whack.

A knock sounded on the door and Nick walked in, holding a printed piece of white paper with the familiar logo of Barago Hospital's pathology department. The smile on his face didn't quite reach his eyes and the lines around his mouth looked strained.

'I brought you this.' He handed the report to Kirby and immediately turned his attention to Melinda. 'I'm Nick Dennison. I hope you don't mind me barging in like this but as I'm working with Dr Atherton I thought I'd introduce myself.'

Recognition moved across the sick woman's face. 'Oh, you're from the market. When I bought those strawberries from you on Saturday I didn't realise you were a doctor. Mind you, I didn't get to taste any of them, the kids ate them all before we got home!'

Kirby heard the warm burr of his voice reply to Melinda but her whirling brain didn't decipher the words. At first astonishment that Nick had brought in the report drowned out the conversation then shock rocked through her, muting everything around her, and finally aching despair obliterated all sound. She read the pathology report three times and finally closed her eyes against the words. But they lingered against her retina as if burned there. Melinda had leukaemia.

Slowly the conversation between Nick and her patient sounded in her ears again and she sucked in a deep breath, turning to face them both. Nick had pulled up a chair, his casual demeanour tinged with an alertness she hadn't noticed before. She realised he'd read the report and that was why he'd brought it in.

She shot him an appreciative look—she hated giving out bad news. It wasn't something a person got better at with practice and it certainly never got easier. 'Melinda, the results of your blood test are back and I'm afraid it's not good news.'

Melinda instantly stiffened, fear clear in her eyes. 'What do you mean?'

Nothing Kirby could say would soften the truth. 'Your white blood cells—the ones that fight infection—are abnormal and that means you have a form of leukaemia.'

Melinda's hand shot to her mouth before falling back to her lap. 'You mean cancer of the blood?'

Kirby nodded slowly. 'That's right. We need to get you to

Barago hospital this afternoon for a series of tests, including a bone-marrow biopsy so that we can get an accurate diagnosis and start chemotherapy.'

But Kirby knew Melinda hadn't heard a word since she'd confirmed leukaemia was cancer.

The petrified woman started to breath quickly, short, shallow breaths, her hands gripping the sides of the chair.

Kirby reached for a paper bag but Nick grabbed it first.

'Melinda.' He squatted down in front of her and took her hand. Looking straight into her eyes, he spoke slowly. 'I need you to breathe into the paper bag and try to slow your breathing. I'm going to count to help you.'

Melinda's gaze fixed on Nick like a drowning woman seeking a life preserver in a choppy sea. Her hands trembled against the paper bag.

The timbre of Nick's voice vibrated reassuringly. 'Breathe in…breathe out… Breathe in…breathe out. That's fabulous, you're doing really well.'

Kirby stood up, needing to do something, and gently touched Melinda's shoulder. 'The dizzy feeling will fade with the deep breaths.' She felt so inadequate. This woman had just been told awful, life-changing news and her battle was only just beginning.

She caught Nick's steady gaze, filled with empathy, but she couldn't see any trace of her own feelings of powerlessness and frustration there. Had he given bad news so often that it no longer got to him? She immediately dismissed the uncharitable thought but she couldn't fathom the rock-solid determination that took up residence in his eyes.

Slowly Melinda lowered the brown paper bag onto her lap, her pupils, large and black, almost obliterating her hazel irises. 'I'm going to die, aren't I?'

Nick kept his hand on Melinda's arm as he sat back in his chair. 'You're about to start the biggest challenge of your life but many people successfully go into remission and go on to lead long and happy lives.'

A sob escaped Melinda's lips. 'But you can't tell me I'm not going to die.'

Nick spoke quietly, his voice steady and firm. 'Right now we don't know enough about your condition to tell you any more than what Kirby already said. This is why you're going to Barago for an accurate diagnosis and then probably to Melbourne for treatment.'

He leaned closer and the dappled sunshine streaming through the window caught his profile, emphasising the silver in his short hair and the unusually deep lines around his eyes and mouth. 'But I can tell you this—leukaemia will test you and force you to dig deep to release a strength you never knew you had. It will make you question everything about your life, force you to prioritise and give you the opportunity to truly know what is important to you.'

Kirby watched Melinda visibly calm under Nick's words and she wished she'd been able to express herself so eloquently but she was still back at 'It's so not fair'. She'd never heard any doctor speak about cancer like that. Usually, it was sticking to the bare facts about treatment.

As he picked up Melinda's hand, sunlight struck the backs of his hands, making the scars whiter than ever. 'I know you didn't put your hand up for this and it's a journey you don't want to take, but I can guarantee you there are parts of the trip that you won't regret.'

'Can I hold you to that?' Melinda's pain-tinged words sliced through the air.

Kirby's heart hurt and anger surged through her that a young mother of three had to deal with this illness and all the unknowns a disease like cancer generated.

'Absolutely, and I'm here to talk to any time.' Nick smiled but, unlike his usual charisma-laden grin, this smile simply conveyed serenity. 'And once you're home, I'll be keeping you supplied with vegetables.'

How could he be so calm? She railed against the unjust diagnosis. Melinda had leukaemia! How on earth could he be talking about vegetables?

Organic vegetables.

Something urged her to really study him while his attention was fully fixed on Melinda and slowly information started to slot into place. He was an experienced city doctor now growing vegetables in the country and avoiding talking about why. His shorter than expected hair grew darker than the blond it had been two years ago and the premature streaks of silver in his hair matched up with the deep lines around his eyes and mouth. White marks on the backs of his hands matched the type of scars left by an intravenous cannula.

Her lungs emptied of air and a shard of pain cramped her heart as all her unanswered questions about Nick lined up. She'd just solved the puzzle. She'd bet her last cent he was talking to Melinda not as a doctor but as a fellow traveller. Nick Dennison had experienced cancer.

The only question still needing an answer was what type of cancer. *No, there's one more. Has he won the battle?*

The thought that he might not terrified her more than it should.

CHAPTER FOUR

NICK bit into the sweet nectarine, savouring the complex but delicious summer flavour on his tongue, and marvelling at the taste. Once he wouldn't have given that a second thought.

'That looks good.' Kirby walked into the staffroom, her usual cheerful demeanour completely absent, dented by the morning's work and Melinda's diagnosis.

This woman confounded him. She lurched from being in charge and confident to needing more reassurance than he would have thought necessary. She reminded him of a junior resident, which was nonsense as she must have far more experience than that if she was doing her first GP rotation.

'Catch.' He tossed her a nectarine and pulled out a chair.

'Thanks.' She bit into the fruit she'd neatly caught and juice dribbled down her chin. Her pink tongue darted out, stroking her skin and licking at the sweet juice.

The image of her tongue against his chin, against his lips, in his mouth, beamed in 3D depth. Colours exploded in his head as blood drained to his groin. He silently started chanting the names of all the bones in the body and blood slowly and regretfully returned to his head.

Now fully back in control, he risked looking at Kirby with

the eyes of a colleague. Right now she needed a mentor and that was his job. He sat down and gave her an encouraging smile. 'If you're going to take everyone's problems on board like this then you're not going to last very long as a GP.'

Her large doe-like eyes reflected sadness, and a sigh rolled over her plump bottom lip. 'But it's just so unfair.'

He took in a thoughtful breath and wondered if she was one of those people who had lived a charmed life untouched by misfortune. 'Life isn't fair, Kirby. Surely you've worked that out by now.'

Her sparkling eyes, always so fill of vibrant colours and movement, suddenly filled with pervading emptiness. The change both startled and disturbed him and something inside him ached.

A moment later she shook her head and gave him a tight smile. 'I know I'm a hopeless case but when something happens outside the realm of what is expected in the circle of life, I find myself railing against it. If Melinda was seventy-eight I'd feel sad but she would have raised her kids and lived a full life.'

Memories of a parade of eyes filled with resignation and expressions of grief and fear hammered him. 'She still can.' His words sounded overly firm but he hated the way people assigned a death certificate to a diagnosis of cancer, which was why he refused to talk about what he'd been through.

A flash of understanding and purpose streaked across her face. 'Oh, don't get me wrong, of course she can and I hope she will, but I wouldn't wish that *struggle* on anyone.' Her gaze hovered on him for a moment, her expression intent. 'Would you?'

The hairs on his arms rose for a moment as he met her unsettling stare. He leaned back casually and placed the pit of his nectarine on a plate that sat between them, striving not to give anything personal away. 'Of course not. But although her treatment will be tough, she'll appreciate parts of the process.'

'Really?' Her brow creased in lines of confusion. 'How so?'

'She'll learn a lot about herself.'

'More than if she wasn't sick?'

He relaxed as the discussion stayed centred on Melinda. 'Absolutely. In general, human beings don't like change and most of us don't put our hand up to experience it. Cancer barges in and railroads you so you have no choice but to meet it head on and change.' He learned forward, warming to his topic. 'You drop the non-essentials and you see things with a clarity not everyone gets the opportunity to have. It's probably the only advantage of the disease.'

'That's an interesting perspective.' Kirby put the pit of the nectarine down on the plate and then leaned forward on her elbows, her chin resting on the palms of her hands, her gaze fixed directly on him. 'I've never heard it explained like that before but that's because it's happened to you, hasn't it? That's why you're here in Port, growing vegetables, instead of slaying even bigger career dragons in Melbourne.'

His chest tightened at her soft-voiced but accurate assumption. Damn it, he'd walked right into her question and he didn't want to answer it. He wanted his time in Port to be free of everything he associated with illness. He didn't want to see sympathy for him shining from those large bluer-than-blue eyes, and he didn't want her to start tiptoeing around him like people had in Melbourne. He just wanted things to be as they had been right up until this point. Shrugging, he bluffed. 'Perhaps I just wanted a tree-change.'

She shook her head. 'I *might* have believed that on Saturday. After all, growing veggies and living in the bush could have been because you'd burned out from years of fast-tracking up the professional ladder, but even then it was a stretch. Now too many things add up—your hair, your vice-less diet.' Her fingers reached out toward his hand and with a feather-soft touch they traced a jagged white scar. 'The marks of an infected IV.'

A fire-storm of sensation detonated under her touch, rolling through him fast and leaving smouldering desire in its wake. Desire he could no longer pretend didn't exist. 'Why is this so important to you, Sherlock?' He trapped her hand with his free one, sandwiching hers between his.

Her pupils dilated into inky discs and a pulse fluttered in her throat as she took a long deep breath, making her breasts strain against the fitted bodice of her dress. 'Because you're a puzzle.'

He recognised her body's response to him, the marks of desire matching those of his own. Their attraction for each other ran between them like a vibrating wire.

It had been months and months since he'd held a woman's hand, hell, since he'd really held a woman. Like so many things in his life, he'd taken for granted the touch of a woman. He loved women. He loved their company, their scent, their curves—everything about them—and now his body craved to hold a woman in his arms again. He ached for it. These feelings he understood. Mutual attraction. Undiluted lust.

And he read them in Kirby's pink cheeks, her slightly open mouth and in the lift of her breasts. He read enough to want the buzz of the chase.

But without warning the heat from her hand surprisingly morphed from scorching fire to cosy heat, warming him, swirling around in sweet tendrils, licking at his self-imposed silence.

'And I can't resist solving puzzles.' She smiled a long, slow, knowing smile, which wound across her face, bringing it alive, the way colour invigorated a black and white canvas.

A smile that promised something good, something wonderful. A smile that called to him unlike any smile ever had. Right there and then, not telling her became harder than keeping his own counsel.

'So you can't resist me?' He traced a circle on her hand with his thumb.

Kirby's body shivered as his caress sent waves of delicious need pounding through her. *Remember Anthony, remember the hurt.* She forced out a laugh and pulled her hand out from under his, ignoring the chill that followed. 'See, this is the puzzle. You're known for flirting charm.'

'But not for growing vegetables. Fair enough.' His guarded expression unexpectedly melted. 'I can see why me being in Port is a puzzle because for years I worked hard and played hard.'

'So what changed?' She tried not to sound as if she was interrogating him but she badly wanted to know what had happened more than she probably should.

'Just under two years ago I couldn't shake off a virus. I felt like I had treacle running through my veins and I was constantly tired and my skin seemed to itch like mad. Then I discovered a pea-sized lump just behind my ear.' He tilted his head, his deep green eyes questioning. 'What do you think, Doctor?'

He'd just turned his story into a teaching session. She ran the symptoms through her mind. 'A type of lymphoma?'

'Well done, Dr Atherton. I had stage-one non-Hodgkin's

lymphoma so I stepped down from Melbourne City and started seven months of IV chemotherapy.'

She schooled her face not to show any emotion but to keep it focussed on a teaching session, as that was obviously the way he wanted to go. 'How was that?'

'What do you think it might be like?'

She spoke from the heart. 'Bloody awful.'

He laughed a rich, body-shaking laugh. 'That pretty much sums it up.' He flattened his hands out against the table. 'And you're pretty observant, Sherlock. I did have problems with infections on my hands so I ended up with a chest tube and a natty scar.'

He raised his brows and shot her a look of pure, unadulterated flirtation—a classic Nick Dennison look. 'But you didn't know that because you're *yet* to see me with my shirt off.'

Her mouth dried at the thought of all that exposed golden skin but despite the fog of lust that encircled her brain she managed to see through his ploy. She rolled her eyes. 'You can't derail me that easily.' *Liar!* 'I want to hear the whole story. Did you have radiation therapy as well?'

He ran his hand through his hair and frustration raced across his face. 'Yeah, I did and losing my hair really sucked, not because I minded being bald for a while but because I realised that when things get to me I run my hand through my hair. When there is no hair to tug on there's no satisfaction in it at all.'

'You could have invented a new action.'

He smiled, his eyes sparkling and dimples scoring his cheeks. 'Ah, but old habits are very hard to break.'

Just like flirting. It was second nature to him—see a woman and flick into flirting mode. 'It won't be long before you can really bury your fingers in your hair.' Her fingers tingled, wanting to do that very thing, and she quickly laced them together. 'But generally treatment takes about seven months. How come you didn't go back to work?'

He pushed back his chair, walked to the water filter and flicked on the tap, pouring two glasses of water. 'I went onto oral chemotherapy and I felt awful. If I'd worked at a desk job perhaps I could have managed it, but not A and E.'

She stood up and walked over to him, calculating the elapsed time since his diagnosis, still confused. 'Are you still on chemo, still battling the lymphoma?'

He immediately stiffened. 'No. The chemo is finished and I'm in remission. I'm not battling non-Hodgkin's lymphoma. I'm surviving it.'

His words shot out harsh and uncompromising and at that moment she understood exactly why he hadn't wanted to talk about being sick. He was focussed on his future, not his past. 'And Port and growing vegetables is part of that?'

He passed her the glass of cold water and leaned back against the bench next to her. 'When you spend a year feeling like death warmed up, you get sick of yourself and you get sick of the role of being a patient. You also get weary of well-intentioned people asking you how you are.' His eyes narrowed slightly, as if willing her to understand and warning her at the same time. 'I wanted some time out between being a patient and going back to work, time to just enjoy being well.'

'But why did you decide to grow vegetables?'

'When you're faced with the possibility of dying, you make changes you never expected to have to make. Taking a break from work was one, changing what I ate was another. Until I got sick it was easy to dismiss the link between food and illness but I can feel the difference in myself. I couldn't do "nothing" for nine months and I was growing my own veggies so I just extended it, and the markets are fun. I came out there because no one up here knew me—' He gave a wry grin, resignation clinging to him. 'Well, almost no one.'

She bit her lip, realising that by pushing him back to work she'd interrupted his plan. 'Sorry.'

He leaned into her, his shoulder nudging hers in a friendly bump and his arm lingering against the length of her own. 'No, don't be sorry, it's all good. I'm enjoying myself and in six months' time when I go back to the city I won't be rusty.'

His body warmth swam through her, making her dizzy. *In six months' time.* At least he had a plan. She'd rushed to Port so fast she really couldn't see past tomorrow. All she knew was that everything she'd expected to be happening in her life right now wasn't. Every plan she and Anthony had made lay scattered in a million irreparable pieces and her love for him had been returned, stamped unacceptable.

Her world spun on an unsteady axis and the only thing about her future that she truly knew was that it would not be happening with Anthony. *Not happening with any man.*

'You OK?' Penetrating eyes bored into her.

She shoved her gloomy thoughts of heart-breaking loss back down where they belonged, plastered a smile on her face and spoke the first thing that came into her head. 'I'm still having trouble seeing you as a farmer.'

'Come see me in action, then.' He pulled his keys out of his pocket and walked toward the door. 'I'm working in the veggie patch every afternoon.'

The unexpected invitation was tantalisingly tempting. She

strove for feigned interest and casualness. 'I'll keep that in mind if I'm ever out that way on rounds.'

He nodded. 'You do that. Around three is a good time to drop by.'

'Is that when you take a break?'

He stared straight at her, his eyes shimmering like sunshine on water, backlit with teasing intent. 'It's the hottest part of the day and usually the time I lose the shirt.' He gave her a knowing wink and disappeared.

Indignation at his perceptive wink, the one that said he knew she enjoyed looking at him, floundered against the surge of hot, delicious longing that shook her to her toes and left her wanting more.

He's your colleague and mentor. But the words sounded hollow. She dragged in a deep breath, determined to make the words count. They had to mean something. They had to protect her because, no matter how much she wanted to see where he lived, no matter how much her body craved to see him shirtless, she wouldn't allow it to happen.

She couldn't. She refused to allow herself to get close to another man again and have him find that her perfect body was so internally flawed. No way was she going to expose her faulty body to any more derision and heartache. She lived with the heartache every day already.

Nick took a long slug of water from his water bottle and then took off his hat and squirted some over his head, enjoying the coolness of the liquid against his hot skin. Turbo gave him a baleful look from under the tree. 'Hot, mate, isn't it? Only mad dogs and Englishmen go out in the midday sun, eh?'

Turbo barked.

'Sorry, I see what you mean. It's three o'clock and you're under the tree so you don't qualify as mad.' He jammed his hat back on his head and toyed with the idea of stopping but he needed to get this fertilising done now that his mornings were taken up with the clinic.

He caught himself glancing down the dirt track that doubled as his driveway. Heat haze hovered, making the metal of the closed gate look crooked. It had been four days since he'd issued his invitation to Kirby, suggesting she visit the farm.

Four days since she'd sat opposite him, her cheeks flushed, glistening lush lips and a sultry voice that rumbled through him every time he thought about it. She hadn't been able to hide her attraction to him and he'd expected her to drive up the track the following day. But she hadn't shown up and she hadn't mentioned the invitation since he'd extended it.

It was probably a good thing. *I don't think so.* He ignored the voice, overlaying it with reason. He'd been high on the joy of lust when he'd issued the invitation and had broken his self-imposed requirement of keeping work and play separate. Two years of celibacy could do that to a bloke.

The professional colleague part of him was pleased that at least she was the one being sensible but despite knowing that he still glanced at the gate each afternoon. It niggled that he did that. It niggled even more that she hadn't come. Two years ago he'd never been stood up and he wasn't that sure he wanted to get used to the feeling.

Two years ago and for years before that he'd dated women—lots of women. He loved the chase, the variety, the conversations and the sex. Unlike his parents, who'd been high-school sweethearts and had married each other at twenty-two, he'd avoided anything that came close to a committed relationship.

And cancer hadn't changed that. A committed relationship meant marriage and children. He didn't particularly have anything against marriage per se, but children, well, no way was he going to be a parent. Not when he'd lived through his parents' unresolved grief—he had no intention of reliving that same nightmare or exposing himself to that sort of loss again.

I just want a normal sister. His twelve-year-old self jetted up from the depths he normally kept sealed.

Plunging his shovel into the enormous pile of mushroom compost, he threw himself into the work and pushed his childhood back where it belonged. But he couldn't get the usual buzz of satisfaction that hard labour gave him because Kirby kept dogging his thoughts. Kirby with a mouth designed for kissing and a body made for pleasure, but who'd been professionally friendly at work and had kept every conversation strictly about patients. No matter what topic he tried to bring up she always neatly brought the conversation back to work. The level of supervision she was demanding bothered him.

By now in her career she really should have a lot more confidence in her diagnostic ability and treatment options, and only be using him as a sounding board for difficult cases. Instead, she seemed to want his review of all her cases. He needed to talk to her about that.

He lifted the shovel, dumping the contents into the wheelbarrow. He'd do it tomorrow but he'd have to be ready because every day this week, at the end of their lunchtime meeting, Kirby had jumped up and said, 'You'd better head off so you can enjoy your afternoon,' and she'd walked briskly out of the staffroom door, back toward her office.

His body absorbed the rhythm of the shovelling, his mind unravelling and roaming free. He suddenly realised that all week Kirby had been leaving the meeting abruptly the moment the last case had been discussed. She never lingered just to chat. No chatting and she hadn't visited. Was it possible she didn't want to spend any time with him?

Nah, not possible.

Laughing at the resurgence of his now healthy if misguided ego, he laid his shovel across the wheelbarrow and lifted the handles, ready to push his load to the vegetable garden.

Turbo barked and jumped up.

'Rest time's over, is it?'

Instead of running over to Nick, Turbo stood stock still, his black ears standing up, alert and listening. He ran part way down the track and then returned, barking all the time as if to say, *Come on.*

Nick put the barrow down and listened. Faintly in the distance he could hear the vroom of an engine. Using his hand as a shield against the sun, he saw a familiar, once-white, now red-dust-covered four-wheel drive round the bend and pull up at the gate.

Everything comes to those who wait. The gorgeous Kirby had arrived and for the first time ever they were going to be truly alone. He couldn't stop the broad smile rolling over his lips.

CHAPTER FIVE

YOU'VE still got time to turn around. Kirby braked at Nick's gate, already regretting the impulsive decision to drive along Nick's road in the hope of checking out his house. Why hadn't she just kept driving straight back into Port? Checking over her shoulder, she threw the gear stick into reverse, anxious to get back to the safety of the main road. With a quick, final glance around to check all areas were clear before she pressed down the accelerator, she looked up—straight into lush-green smiling eyes filled with a wicked glint.

Nick. Her mouth dried, and her tongue automatically moistened her lips. He'd seen her and now there was no turning back.

He moved forward with the easy grace of a panther and with a practised hand lazily swung the gate open and walked toward her car, his gait easy and rolling—a farmer's walk complete with a faithful dog trotting by his side. This time he really did look like a farmer from the tip of his battered hat down to his worn elastic-sided boots. Thankfully a shirt still covered his chest but as he got closer she realised it was wet.

Damp cotton clung to well-defined pectoral muscles and solid biceps, outlining them in perfect, taunting detail. Her heart thundered so hard in her chest that she could hear it. Could he? For all that the shirt didn't hide, it may as well have been off. *Why* had she pulled the wheel hard right at Sheep-Wash Corner? After all, her concern about a patient could have waited until tomorrow morning.

But that's not really why you're here, is it? You caved in and gave in to wanting to see where he lived. Gave in to wanting to see him.

Her palm connected hard with the top of the steering wheel and she welcomed the jarring sensation thudding painfully all the way to her shoulder. She was really starting to hate that challenging voice. She knew she should have just kept driving but she hadn't so now she needed to salvage the situation.

Wanting to be on the front foot, she flicked the switch that operated her window and watched it wind down, determined to get in the first word. 'Hello.'

He leaned forward, his arms resting casually on the door. 'G'day. Glad you could make it.'

His slow, drawling delivery stroked her skin, stoked the banked heat inside her. She swallowed hard as his scent of rich earth, hard work and soap washed over her, tugging at a basic need. In her search for control she blurted out, 'I was on my way back from visiting Tom Lenders and I wanted to ask you something.'

Dark brows rose, overriding the first crease of a frown as a flicker of disquiet appeared in his eyes. He pushed back from the door, the corded muscles in his arms thick like rope. 'Put her in gear and I'll meet you up at the house.'

'Are you sure?'

He nodded and slapped the cab of the vehicle with his hand as if to say, *Go through now*.

With her gut churning she drove through the gate, but Turbo soon had her smiling as he bounded forward, racing the car up past an enormous fenced vegetable garden. Glancing in the rear-view mirror, she saw Nick swing and latch the gate shut before turning and jogging back along the track. Pulling her eyes back to the road, she took the curve and a house came into view.

Wonder chased by regret immediately poured through her. A freshly painted weatherboard miner's cottage with a corrugated-iron roof stood in front of her, its plain Victorian lines offset by the simple decorative carving at the top of each veranda post. She slipped out of the four-wheel drive, her feet crunching on gravel, and Turbo immediately dropped a ball at her feet, panting at her in enthusiastic anticipation.

Distracted, she patted his head, her gaze still fixed on the house. *Whatever you want, my darling. Nothing will ever be too much for my wife and family. You know family is everything to me.*

She swallowed hard against Anthony's duplicitous voice and walked slowly up the box-hedge-lined path that led to the centre of the veranda and the front door flanked by matching aloe vera plants in heritage green wooden planters. Her shoes sounded loud on the hardwood boards as she stepped up from the worn bluestone step. Two wicker chairs sat invitingly on the veranda, with a low table in front of them. A sheaf of papers had been weighted down by a jug covered with an old-fashioned doily that kept flies from touching the contents. A well-thumbed novel lay face down, its spine deeply creased down the centre.

If there'd been a discarded scooter or skateboard nearby and some balls and a chalkboard, it would have been exactly as she'd pictured the house Anthony had promised her. The one she'd envisaged sharing with him and raising their family in.

Don't go there. Anthony doesn't want you. It's over, you know it's over.

Taking a deep breath, she plastered a smile on her face and turned at the sound of Nick's footsteps on the crushed white-rock path. 'Great house.'

'Thanks. I like it, although I wouldn't want to spend a winter without installing some heating.' He grinned at her. 'Open fires are all very romantic but they don't keep you very warm. It's definitely a summer house.'

He pulled off his work gloves, dropped them onto the table and poured two glasses of what looked like lemon cordial from the jug and passed her a glass. 'Grab a seat.'

Tendrils of warmth flicked through her veins as she lowered herself into the wide, comfortable chair. 'Is that the plan after this summer? To use it as a holiday house?'

He leaned back in his chair, his long legs stretching out in front of him, his left arm hanging down the side of the chair as his fingers rubbed Turbo's head. 'Probably. I love it down here but, like you, it's just a short-term plan.'

She stiffened as the horror of returning to Melbourne merged with all her insecurities. 'Why would you assume my plan is short term? Don't you think I can cut it as a country GP?'

He levelled a prosaic stare directly at her. 'You said this was your first GP rotation. That means you have to do a second one somewhere else.'

'Oh, right.' *Dumb, dumb, dumb.* She really should learn to think before she spoke. She took a slug of her drink and changed the subject. 'This is delicious—what is it?'

'Home-made lemon cordial.' He trailed his finger around the rim of his glass. 'You said you wanted to ask me something about Tom Lenders?'

Thankful to be back on safe territory she grabbed onto the topic with enthusiasm. 'Tom is a seventy-five-year-old man with hypertension and has recently been complaining of shortness of breath.'

'Any history of asthma?'

'No, and his chest X-ray is clear. There's no sign of cardiomyopathy or congestive cardiac failure but he has an audible wheeze and his peak flow is lower than expected.'

He tilted his head, intelligent eyes scanning her. 'So, what are *your* thoughts?'

She sat a bit straighter, feeling confident of her answer. 'I'm thinking that he has a form of asthma precipitated by the betablocker he's been taking for four years.'

Frown lines formed across his brow. 'And you brought this case to review why?'

She caught the slight tone of censure and was puzzled by his reaction. 'I wanted to be sure I didn't miss anything.'

He nodded, his lips pursing together firmly. 'You haven't missed a thing *but* I think you're missing the hospital system.'

His words sailed far too close to the truth for comfort and she smiled tightly. 'It takes a bit of getting used to but, no, I wouldn't say I was missing it.'

One black eyebrow rose enquiringly. 'Really? You've come from an environment where every decision made by a resident is reviewed by the registrar and every decision made by the registrar is reviewed by the consultant.' He put down his glass. 'Although by the time third year's over, most consultants are giving registrars a large amount of free rein.'

'Hmm.' She nodded and tacitly agreed. After all, what he said was true even though it hadn't actually happened to her.

He leaned forward. 'You would have found that?'

His gaze seemed to rivet itself to her mouth and she realised she was gnawing her bottom lip. She *so* didn't want to talk about this. Didn't want talk about how her life had fallen apart and she'd left her position at Prince William's way too early.

She tried a politician's tactic. Nodding, she gave another 'Hmm' and raised her arm. 'What do you call that tree over there?'

His head didn't move and his eyes didn't even flicker in the direction of the solid tree with the unusual seedpods. 'A banksia.' His gaze narrowed and his jaw tightened. 'You did finish third year?'

His accusatory tone lingered between them and his razor-sharp investigative look not only cornered her, it pinned her to the wall. Every instinct had her wanting to flee and she willed her phone to ring, wanting something, anything, to happen that would get her out of here. Adrenaline poured through her, the fight-and-flight response going into over-drive, and her body responded violently with a flush of non-sexual heat.

Horrible, unwanted heat washed through her, starting in her toes and building in intensity until all her skin burned so hot and tinder dry it felt like it would peel. Sweat immediately followed—drenching her, running in rivulets under her breasts, settling in the creases of her skin, threatening to soak her vest top. She gave thanks it was a hot summer's day and the flush and sweating would go unnoticed.

You're twenty-seven! What did you do to make this happen? Anthony's bitter voice boomed in her head. She downed her drink, forcing away the unwelcome voice, willing the hot flush to subside and steeling herself against the painful reminder of what it really meant.

Nick rose in one fluid movement and silently refilled her glass before settling back into his chair. His quiet voice rumbled deeply around the veranda, laced with tough resolve. 'As I'm acting as your mentor, I need to know how much experience you really have. You need to be honest with me, Kirby. I need the truth.'

The truth. Her heart pounded in agitation. He'd caught her out. She'd been double-checking everything because she hadn't had enough experience as a senior medical officer. But the moment she told him she'd left Prince William's early he'd ask why and the truth involved so many things she didn't want to tell.

The truth, the whole truth and nothing but the truth. The words read to a witness in court echoed in her mind. Suddenly a tiny shaft of light pierced the darkness and she knew she could tell Nick the truth. She sent up a silent vote of thanks that he hadn't asked for the whole truth. That she wasn't prepared to give.

Nick waited, watching a battle of emotions on Kirby's oval face. She really didn't want to tell him but he wouldn't let her get away without telling him. He would have to write up a report on her and for an accurate assessment he needed to have a starting benchmark. But he didn't want to sound like an inquisitor.

After all, she'd come out here to visit and he wanted it to be social more than work. He wanted a chance to be alone with her. He stood up and extended his hand. 'How about we walk and talk? There's a place I'd like to show you.'

Her already large eyes seemed to expand and her pale face flickered with gratitude mixed with resistant resignation. 'If you insist.' Her hand slowly slid into his.

'I do.' He pulled her to her feet and her reluctance seeped slowly into him, tagged by slowly building heat.

The moment she stood, she eased her hand out of his and walked toward the veranda steps.

Inexplicable loss streaked through him and he forced down every desire to grab back her hand. He strode after her. 'This way—the path goes from the back of the house.'

They walked in silence for a few minutes and he finally broke it. 'Come on, Sherlock, fill me in.'

She ducked under a low branch of a casuarina tree, her footfall hushed against the pile of dropped needles. 'You're right. I didn't finish my third year. In fact, I only completed seven months.'

He held up another branch for her and gave in to his need to breathe deeply, inhaling her wildflower scent as she passed by. 'That goes some way to explaining things.'

She gave a tight smile. 'Good.'

With the set of her mouth and the line of her shoulders he knew she was holding back more than she was giving. He took a calculated gamble to get her to tell him the story. 'Were you asked to leave Prince William?'

She came to an abrupt halt, indignation streaking across her face. 'No, I was not asked to leave. In fact, I was asked to reconsider my resignation.'

'But you didn't.'

'No.' She sighed and kept walking. 'I left for personal reasons.'

The path ended as they arrived at a creek lined with vibrant green tree ferns. Large fronds bent low toward the water, which burbled and rushed over and around granite boulders worn smooth by its action. Getting Kirby to tell him her story was like getting blood from one of the creek's stones. 'They must have been pretty big reasons if you left a job to come to this one before you were one hundred per cent ready.'

Her hands balled into fists and hung by her sides. 'If breaking off an engagement constitutes big, I guess it was.'

Her words surprised him, mostly because he hadn't expected her to have been engaged. He'd never considered marriage, it wasn't part of his life's plan, but he could empathise. 'At least you broke it off before it involved the full catastrophe of property and children.'

She swung away from him, an agonising sound starting to break from her lips.

The sound stopped abruptly but not before it tore at something inside him. He reached out and touched her arm. 'Hell, Kirby, I'm sorry, I just assumed it was you who broke it off.'

She turned back slowly toward him, her expression so full of hurt that it was the most natural thing in the world to pull her into his arms. With his forefinger he traced a line down her cheek. 'He didn't deserve you.'

As she looked up at him her voice cracked. 'He didn't want me the way I am.'

More than anything he wanted to banish the look of empty desolation that hovered in her beautiful eyes, haunting him. He tipped his head forward, feeling the caress of her breath on his face. 'More fool him.'

She stared straight at him and snagged her bottom lip with her teeth.

Desire thundered through him so hard it almost knocked the breath from his lungs. With his hand gently cupping her jaw, he lowered his mouth to hers, fusing his lips against her waiting softness and claiming what he'd dreamed about for days. She tasted of sugar tinged with citrus, of searing heat and need, and he lost himself in her, like a parched man stumbling into an oasis.

He trailed his tongue across her lips, touching, tasting and seeking entry, needing to bury himself in her heat and tang. Needing to absorb her essence, feel it in his veins.

Her mouth opened slowly under his and with a moan of need he accepted her unspoken invitation and deepened the kiss. Like an early voyager he explored and then he plundered, eagerly taking everything and still not getting enough. His arms tightened around her, moulding her soft curves to his toned body, treasuring the feel of having a beautiful, supple woman in his arms again. Stunned by how it far exceeded any memory.

Pulling away the loose band that barely held her hair in place, he breathed deeply, taking his fill of the aroma of cinnamon apples. His fingers splayed through her silky strands, revelling in the way their softness caressed his skin. As his mouth played over hers, he explored all the contours and dips, the peaks and hollows and left behind a firm imprint of himself.

The sound of the racing water of the creek, the songs of the birds and the rustling of the breeze through the ferns slowly retreated. All that existed was the feel of Kirby in his arms, the touch of her mouth against his and the way his blood pounded through him until every cell vibrated with the bliss of being alive.

'Nick.'

Her voice seemed a long way away. 'Hmm?' He started to trail kisses down to her jaw.

'Nick.' Her voice sounded louder, insistent, and her hands gripped his upper arms.

The pressure acted like a brake. He lifted his head and looked at her through dazed eyes, her image slowly coming into focus. Her fine hair cascaded around her face in complete disarray, her lush lips were wet, pink and swollen, but it was the startled look in her eyes that centred him with thudding brutality.

What the hell had he just done? He'd always prided himself on his finesse with women, of giving rather than taking, and yet right now, without any thought for her or her comfort, he'd kissed her senseless like a frustrated and randy teenager. He pulled back, mortified. 'I'm sorry, I shouldn't have done that. I shouldn't have kissed you.'

She stiffened slightly and her eyes, normally so clear, suddenly clouded, but then she shook her head. 'Please don't feel bad, it's not you, it's me. I just can't do this right now.' She drew in an unsteady breath and rested her palm on his forearm. 'I know it sounds really clichéd but what I really need is for you to be a colleague and a friend.'

A friend.

His blood drained from his groin and tried to perfuse his brain. A beautiful woman stood in front of him asking for his friendship. He'd never really done friendship with a woman and every part of him recoiled. He wanted her in his arms, he wanted her naked, and he wanted her wrapped tightly around him. Hell, he just wanted her.

He silently cursed the complete irony of the situation. His body had finally come roaring back to life, pulsing with virile good health, and the one woman he wanted didn't want him.

Somehow he managed to smile. 'Sure, I understand.'

Relief streamed across her face. 'You do?'

'I do.'

The hell you do, he told himself.

But he had to pretend he did. He had no other choice.

CHAPTER SIX

'HEY, Dr Kirby, I bet you I can race you to those big trees.' Cooper pointed to the large Norfolk pines at the far end of the big asphalt car park at the back of Kids' Cottage.

'You're on.' Kirby stooped down and tightened her shoelaces, smiling to herself. Three days ago Cooper had been withdrawn and sullen but the Port sunshine and the fabulous staff at KC had drawn him out. 'But do I get a handicap?'

Cooper flexed his fingers which extended from gloved palms. 'Nah, that's mine and today I'm not sharing.'

She grinned at the determination on his face. 'You're a tough opponent.' She put her left foot forward on an imaginary line as Cooper dropped his hands. 'Ready, set.'

'Go!' Cooper thrust forward, the wheels of his wheelchair spinning quickly as he propelled himself down the slight incline and toward the trees.

Kirby ran hard, needing to put in some serious effort to keep up, and she arrived at the pines seconds after him, panting for breath.

A beaming boy full of the flush of a win gave her faint praise. 'You did OK, Doc, better than my camp counsellor. I beat him by heaps!'

Too breathless to laugh, she rested her hands against her thighs. 'Thanks, Cooper, I like to keep fit.' She caught her breath and then headed back toward the main building, leaving Cooper at the archery range. Glancing at her watch, she increased her pace as she'd promised to do story time for the younger campers.

She loved spending time at KC and couldn't understand why Nick didn't want to do any work here. Why he really preferred not to work with children at all. She wondered if it was because Melbourne City was so very close to the Royal Children's Hospital so not many children came through Emergency. Perhaps he hadn't worked with many kids and paediatrics put him out of his comfort zone. But that reason didn't quite gel with her because Nick Dennison had a bring-it-on attitude to life and nothing seemed to faze him.

It really shouldn't bother her but it nagged at her because it was yet another part of the unsolved puzzle that was Nick, and she hated to admit it but the man fascinated her. He shouldn't because he wasn't her type at all. No man could be her type now.

Still, Nick not wanting to work at KC meant she didn't have to share the kids with anyone. She treasured that, visiting most days, even when she wasn't needed for her professional services. Although there was a large group of diabetic children visiting this week, not all the kids had a medical condition and many campers came to give their parents a break and a chance to sort out issues in their own lives. Often these children needed a lot more TLC than the kids who had a medical condition they'd grown to accept.

She loved children—loved their unbridled enthusiasm, their abundant curiosity and the sheer joy they could get from the simplest things. Her work here kept her busy, but it also kept her sane, filling a big hole in her life, filling a need.

Nick fills a need.

Nick. A vivid image of sea-green eyes filled with the simmering heat of desire flooded her, making her swallow hard.

Two weeks had passed since she'd called at Riversleigh and visited Nick at home. Two weeks since he'd kissed her senseless, reducing her to a quivering mass of pulsating need that had driven every coherent thought from her head. She'd revisited that kiss every day from every angle, from every blissful touch. She'd lost herself completely—melting into his arms and giving herself over to the intoxicating way his mouth had roamed deliciously over hers, sparking trails of glorious sensation that had spun and wove, tantalising her until she'd vibrated with pleasure and yearned for more.

Pathetically, it had only taken the touch of one kiss for her to ignore every promise she'd made to herself. She'd caved in completely and returned his kiss with the fervour of a lust-struck adolescent and taken as much from him as she could get. She'd absorbed his touch, savoured his earthy taste and revelled in the cocoon of his arms, never wanting the kiss to end.

But as the pressure of his mouth had lessened and his lips had trailed gloriously along her jaw, the slight change in his touch had been enough for a tiny but rational fissure to pierce her desire-fuelled haze. Panic had immediately surged. She'd pulled back, half hating what she was doing but knowing it was the right thing.

No matter how she'd once imagined her life playing out, she knew that dream was dead and that getting involved with any man was impossible. She knew that to be an irrefutable truth just as she knew the world to be round. She couldn't offer a man the future he would want—a future that she longed for but knew could never happen.

That was why Anthony had trashed her heart and left her, and why all other men would eventually leave her too. No way was she ever risking her bruised and shattered heart again to such wrenching pain.

Instead, she threw herself into caring for kids because it was as close as she was going to get to a child of her own.

She opened the library door to shrieks of, 'Read this one, Kirby,' and four enthusiastic pre-schoolers mobbed her, each clutching their own choice of book. Laughing, she collapsed onto the bright cushions and beanbags and gathered the children in close. 'We can read them all. Let's start with this story about the hare and his nut-brown baby.'

Warm bodies snuggled in, heads rested on her shoulders and her lap, and podgy hands touched her. She breathed in deeply, knowing intrinsically that she needed the comforting touch of these children as much as they needed her time and care.

The loud clang of metal against metal roused them all from their fourth story. Kirby finished reading the sentence, placed a bookmark between the pages and closed the book. 'That's the dinner bell, gang. Let's skip to the dining hall.'

'I want to hop.' A small but determined five-year-old stood with her hands authoritatively on her hips.

Kirby smiled and adopted a mediating approach. 'We can do that too but maybe we should hold hands.'

With lots of giggles and squeals, they made their way across the quadrangle to the mess hall, where the girls' camp counsellor waited to take them into dinner. 'Wash your hands first.'

As the girls obediently lined up at the taps at the base of

the stairs, the counsellor smiled at Kirby. 'Thanks for doing story-time. It gave me a chance to telephone their parents and reassure them that all is well.'

A real sense of community rolled through her. 'It's my pleasure. I think I enjoy the stories more than they do.' She glanced at her watch. 'But I'd better get going or else the supermarket will be closed and I'm getting tired of tinned spaghetti on toast.'

With a quick wave to the girls, Kirby ducked behind the old, grey, salt-weathered buildings and made her way back toward her car. She'd just pressed the auto-unlock button when she heard someone call her name and she turned toward the voice.

Hurrying toward her was Judy Dalton, the woman in charge of KC, her round cheeks pink with exertion. 'Oh, I'm so glad I caught you. Ben Hadley, one of the diabetic boys, has just vomited everywhere and he's looking a bit pale and wan.'

'Vomiting before dinner? Has he had his before-dinner insulin?' Kirby opened the boot and pulled out her medical kit, a thread of concern weaving through her.

Judy gave a quick nod. 'Yes, he'd just come up to sick bay to have it, which is why I left Phillipa with him, trying to encourage him to eat a jelly snake, and I ran to catch up with you.'

'I'm glad you caught me.' Kirby slammed the boot closed, hoping she could reach the boy before he had a hypo.

They jogged to the sick bay and found thirteen-year-old Ben lying on the bed, his face very white—even his freckles looked pale. Beads of sweat lined his forehead, dripping into his hair, and he'd pulled his legs up under his chin. Shaking, he gripped a large monometal bowl and promptly vomited into it.

'That's the third time he's vomited.' Phillipa quickly exchanged the bowl for a clean one. 'He can't have much more left in his stomach.'

Kirby pulled out her glucometer machine. 'I gather he wasn't able to hold down the snake.'

The woman shook her head. 'No, that came up too.'

'Hey, mate, sorry you're feeling sick.' Kirby knelt down beside Ben and put her hand on his forehead, her fingers hot from the heat radiating from his skin. 'Because you've vomited just after having insulin we need to give you some glucose to prevent a hypo. I'm going to put in a drip so you don't get dehydrated, and when your blood-sugar levels are sorted, we'll work out what's making you sick, OK?'

'OK.' The word came out in the familiar resigned tone that kids with chronic medical conditions often used.

'Finger jab first.' Kirby gave Ben a reassuring smile, quickly pricked his finger and carried out the glucometer reading. As expected, his blood sugar was too low. 'I'm going to give you mini-dose glucagon injection and then insert the drip.'

'My stomach really hurts.' Ben tensed up as a spasm hit him.

Kirby chewed her lip and swallowed a sigh. Vomiting in children could be due to so many different things—appendicitis, urinary-tract infection, meningitis. The list ran through her head as she injected the glucagon so the insulin had something to work on.

'Phillipa, can you please take Ben's temperature with the ear thermometer while I insert the IV?' Kirby handed the instrument to the woman and quickly primed the IV tubing.

'Thirty-nine point one.' Phillipa tossed the disposable earpiece into the bin.

'I thought he felt hot.' Kirby added an antipyretic to her list of drugs for Ben. Wrapping the tourniquet around his arm, she quickly found a vein, which was reassuring as often kids dehydrated really quickly. 'Hold still, Ben, it will be over in a moment.' She slid the IV cannula home and turned the drip onto a medium rate and gave him some Maxalon for the vomiting. 'Right, well, that combined with the rescue dose of glucagon should keep your blood-sugar level above five as well as keeping you hydrated. I've given you something to help the nausea and the fever but now I need to examine you. Tell me where your tummy hurts.'

'Everywhere.' Ben's voice broke on a sob.

She stroked his forehead. 'You poor old thing. I just need to have a gentle feel, OK?' Lifting his T-shirt, she started a gentle palpation of his abdomen, half expecting to find some guarding and rebound tenderness on the right side. Acute appendicitis presented with fever, vomiting and pain.

'Kirby.' Judy walked into the room, supporting a boy who was shivering violently. 'We've got another customer.' She laid the boy down on the other bed in the room. 'This is Cameron and he's diabetic as well.'

'I'm gonna puke.' Cameron heaved.

With the skill of experience Kirby managed to push a bowl under his chin just in time. She wiped his mouth and gave him a sip of water. 'When did you start to feel sick?'

'During dinner.' The boy laid his head back down on the pillow.

Kirby took his temperature. 'Thirty-eight five. You've got a fever, just like Ben. I need to check your blood-sugar levels, OK?'

'I can do it.' Cameron tried to sit up and fell back.

'Are you feeling dizzy?' Kirby asked the rhetorical

question as she quickly pricked his finger. Deftly placing the drop of blood neatly on the stick, she inserted it into the machine. 'Two point seven. I'm giving you a glucagon injection into your thigh right now.'

But Cameron was too drowsy to reply.

'Judy, can you do a glucometer check on Ben for me while I insert a drip into Cam?'

Judy nodded. 'Sure. Do you think they've both picked up a virus? They're in the same bunkhouse.'

Kirby concentrated on locating a vein. 'I had thought Ben might have appendicitis but his examination doesn't match up with that and now with Cameron I'm wondering if—'

Phillipa rushed in. 'I've got four more boys, all with the same symptoms.'

Kirby taped Cameron's IV in place, a sense of foreboding settling in her chest. 'Are they all diabetic?'

'Yes.'

She had kids dropping like flies. Running her hand through her hair, she marshalled her thoughts. 'Is anyone else at camp other than the diabetics starting to get sick?'

Phillipa shook her head. 'Everyone else is hale and hearty, chowing down to dinner as usual.'

She turned to Ben, who was more alert than Cameron. 'Ben, have you eaten anything today that didn't come from the KC kitchen?'

Guilt streaked across his cheeks and he dropped his gaze. 'Maybe.'

Kirby kept her voice light. 'I need you to tell me, mate, so I can work out what is making you and the other boys so sick.'

'I had…I ate a chocolate bar.' The mumbled words were barely audible. 'I'm sorry, I didn't think it would make me hurl.'

She patted his arm. 'I don't think a chocolate bar would cause you to be this sick. Did you eat anything else?'

The sick boy's gaze darted between Kirby, Judy and Phillipa, anxiety and fear duelling with a need to tell the truth. 'We...we sneaked out to the Greasy Spoon.'

Kirby recognised the name of the take-away shop about half a kilometre away and suppressed a sigh. 'Who's "we"?'

He swallowed hard. 'Unit C.'

'And what did you eat?'

'Chicken and chips. The lady gave it to us cheap.'

A vision of hot food sitting in an old bain-marie for longer than the allowed time took residence in Kirby's mind. A cooling chicken would be the perfect vehicle for hosting salmonella. And the boys had the vomiting, nausea and abdominal pain that fitted the picture. She suppressed a groan at the thought of the diarrhoea that would inevitably follow.

She swung around to Judy. 'So we have six boys so far. How many boys are in that bunkhouse?'

Judy grimaced. 'Fourteen.'

'Fourteen?' She couldn't keep the rising inflection of horror out of her voice. Fourteen vomiting diabetics. Fourteen kids at risk of hypoglycaemia. Not to mention other members of the public who might have eaten at the shop. Her mind started to race with the logistics of dealing with this outbreak.

The hospital only had six acute beds and based on what had happened so far they could expect more than double the current number of cases. She needed to set up an isolation ward, get extra medical supplies from Barago and organise an urgent courier to rush samples to the lab for an accurate diagnosis. As Port's medical officer she had to notify the health department and shut down the Greasy Spoon pending investigation and testing. But most importantly she would probably be treating and monitoring fourteen really sick children. Their care came first. How the hell was she going to divide herself up to meet every demand?

Judy and Phillipa looked at her expectantly. 'So what's your plan and how can we help?'

Nick dangled his legs over the edge of the Port Bathurst pier, a fishing rod in one hand and the other resting on Turbo's collar. The dog was crouched down, calculating how to round up the seagulls who hovered close by, ever hopeful of a free feed.

'Fishing is supposed to be relaxing, Turbo. You have to give in to the joy of sitting and waiting.'

Quizzical brown eyes met his gaze and Nick gave an ironic laugh. 'Yeah, well, that's the theory.'

Con Papadopoulos, one of his nursing-home patients, had told him that the pier at the turn of the tide was *the* place to catch dusky flathead. Fishing wasn't something that Nick had ever really done but right now he was looking for new experiences, looking for anything that took his mind off a blue-eyed, blonde-haired beauty with a smile that sent his blood racing.

Fishing didn't seem to be cutting it. Neither had cold showers, ten-K runs or fifty-K bike rides. No matter what he did, thoughts of Kirby roamed wild and free in his mind. He was used to getting what he wanted with women and the fact that she didn't want him in her bed ate at him.

Friendship. The word tasted bitter in his mouth. How could she only want friendship when their desire for each other vibrated palpably between them?

He reeled in the line for the fifth time to find the hook bait-less yet again. He sighed—so far he'd only managed to feed the fish and feed them well. He opened the bait box to try again and his phone vibrated in his pocket. Wiping his hands on his jeans first, he pulled out the phone, a crazy jolt of joy making his heart skip when he read the display. *Kirby.*

Kirby ringing at six o'clock when clinic was over and the evening was looming—perhaps she'd had a change of heart. Pressing the phone to his ear, he answered the call. 'If you're offering to take me out to dinner, I accept because not one single fish has landed on my line.'

'It's not a dinner invitation.'

The serious tone of her voice quickly dispatched all ideas of flirting and he immediately shot into professional mode. 'What's happened?'

'I need you out at Kids' Cottage—'

He cut her off, memories from his childhood flashing at him like a neon sign. 'I told you I don't work at the camp.'

'Well, today you do.' Her voice unexpectedly whipped him. 'I've got a suspected outbreak of salmonella poisoning and so far all the cases are diabetics.'

Hell! He raked his free hand through his hair as his pulse picked up. Sick diabetic kids. This was more than just maintaining fluids and electrolytes. This was complicated by either hyper- or hypoglycaemia. It didn't matter which way he looked at it, didn't matter how he felt about the camp, Kirby was right. This time he didn't have the luxury of choice. As a doctor he had to be there.

Forcing down uncomfortable memories, he sighed. 'I'll be there in ten minutes.'

'Make it five.'

The phone went dead, the silence deafening in its censure.

CHAPTER SEVEN

THE sharp electronic beep of Nick's watch signalled three a.m. as he walked slowly and softly along the long row of beds, the old wooden floorboards creaking in protest as he checked all their patients. Low night lighting illuminated the beds along with the silvery beams of a waning moon and he didn't need to use his torch.

Every bed was predictably identical, although these beds with their laminated pine bedheads and built-in drawers underneath the mattress were a lot more flash than the old metal beds he'd slept on at similar camps around the country. The same brightly coloured doonas lay on each of the eighteen beds and fourteen of them had sick pubescent boys huddled underneath, fitfully sleeping. Four beds contained sick adults who'd also eaten at the Greasy Spoon, their pale faces looking slightly at odds with the 'superpowers' doona tucked under their chins.

Kirby had created an isolation ward in one of the dormitories in the grounds of KC and everyone affected by the outbreak was being treated here rather than at the hospital. It made sense seeing that he and Kirby had been frantic—treating children non-stop for the last nine hours. They'd just managed to go one full hour without admitting a new case and hopefully no one else in the community had eaten the contaminated food.

They'd divided the care of the patients evenly and both of them had been so busy they'd hardly spoken to each other all night, but he'd known exactly where she'd been in the dorm at all times. Her sweet scent wafted on the air and when she spoke to her patients he could hear her reassuring and gentle voice. An immature part of him wished he was sick so he could feel her hand on his brow and hear such care for him in her voice. He ignored the thought as he'd learned long ago to take no notice of errant thoughts generated by long hours and fatigue.

Kirby's manner with the kids was the perfect blend of caring mother and objective professional and he couldn't help but be impressed. *The cottage was a big drawcard for me to come to Port.* He wondered if he should talk to her about pursuing paediatrics.

Judy Dalton touched his arm. 'Phillipa and I are back from a break. I've just convinced Kirby she needs to take one and so do you.'

Nick looked up the dorm toward Cameron.

Judy followed his gaze, understanding on her face. 'I promise I'll call you if he needs you.' She gave him a gentle push. 'Go.'

'You've got my mobile number?'

She nodded patiently. 'You're not going to be far away and I've got your number plus my phone is on and charged. Worst-case scenario, I can yell really loud.' She pointed to the door and mouthed, 'Go now.'

Part of him felt he should stay but most of him wanted to

take the chance of leaving the claustrophobic brown walls of the dorm. He hadn't had a break since he'd arrived.

'You OK?' Kirby greeted him as he walked into the kitchen, her voice soft.

'Fine.' Nick avoided meeting her far-too-observant gaze as he accepted the proffered mug of hot, steaming tea. Instead he stuck to the much easier topic of medical supplies. 'Has more saline arrived from the hospital yet?'

'Theo just rang and it's on its way.' She stifled a yawn but she couldn't hide the dark smudges under her eyes.

'You look completely whacked.' His hand tightened around the mug, tensing against the powerful urge to wrap his arms around her and pull her against him while he stroked her hair and let her sleep on his shoulder.

Her brows rose as her mouth twitched. 'I'd heard you had a way with words.' Laughter threaded through her voice. 'Now I can see why women lined up to date you.' She rested her chin against her palm. 'You look pretty exhausted yourself. How are your boys doing?'

'Fair.' He sipped his tea, welcoming the comforting warmth. Being inside the dorm had brought back far too many uneasy memories—massive homesickness, feelings of abandonment—and Cameron's grip on his hand and the baleful look in his eye had reminded him too much of himself at that age.

He leaned back and swung his feet up onto a chair. 'It's a fine line between too much and not enough insulin, and Cameron's levels keep swinging but at least he's stopped vomiting. I'll be a lot happier when Barago rings in the blood results.'

'Hypernatraemia is always a worry, isn't it?' She slid a covered plate toward him, a plume of steam curling up from the hole in the top of the silver cover. The aroma of garlic and onions filled the room.

He smiled at her rhetorical question that a couple of weeks ago would have been a real question. He was really pleased that she'd started trusting her judgement rather than second-guessing every decision. 'It is. We'll do another round of bloods at six a.m. and check everyone's electrolytes, including potassium.' He lifted up the food cover, suddenly hungry, realising it had been hours since he'd eaten.

She gave a quiet chuckle as she tucked into her spaghetti bolognaise. 'Poor Constable Masterton. This is his first posting after graduation and I think he came to Port hoping to crack an international abalone ring, and we've got him transporting blood samples between here and Barago.'

'Hey, he got to use the siren so he's happy.' Nick couldn't fault the way Port had pulled together to deal with this crisis. The paramedics had transported equipment, the nurses had all come back on duty and spread themselves between the hospital and KC, and now the camp kitchen was working all night keeping the staff well fed.

But it had been Kirby who'd organised everything. 'Three weeks ago I would have doubted you could have handled this sort of challenge but you've aced it. You're one hell of an organiser—I doubt anyone would have been brave enough to say no to you.'

'You tried.' She tilted her head and stared straight at him, her eyes lit with undisguised curiosity. 'I don't get it. Why haven't you wanted to work here?'

Damn it, how had a compliment to her suddenly become all about him? He tried a flippant response. 'You love kids so I was giving you free rein.'

Her stunning eyes narrowed. 'You don't like kids?'

He willed his facial muscles to adopt a neutral expression. 'I don't have anything against them.'

A ripple of irritation skated across her cheeks. 'What sort of answer is that? I saw you in action tonight and you were thorough and caring so I know that you not wanting to work here has *nothing* to do with a lack of medical knowledge, unless…'

He caught the moment her mind made the connection and his stomach clenched.

Her forehead creased with an expression of complete bewilderment. 'Why wouldn't you want to work at a wonderful place like this?'

His sister Sarah's contorted face, her contracted muscles and wasted body beamed through his brain, taking him back twenty-odd years in an instant, the images clogging his mind. His heart hammered against his ribs as voices-past jumbled in his head, loud and discordant.

Your mother needs a break, Nick. This way everyone gets a holiday.

I hate it here, let me come home.

Sweetheart, we love you. Camp will be fun.

'Nick. Nick?'

Kirby's voice broke through the cacophony of sound as he became aware of the clink of the spoon against china. 'You've gone all white. Here, I've added some sugar to your tea.' She pushed the mug into his right hand and covered his left hand with her own. 'It's KC, isn't it?'

She'd done it again. For years he'd spent a lot of time with a lot of women and not one of them had read him like Kirby could. She managed to get under his guard every single time. Her warmth trailed through him, slowing his racing heart, calming him. He finally met her gaze, the pull of her concern drawing him in. 'Yeah, it's the camp, Sherlock. Not this camp specifically but all camps like it. I spent a lot of time in them as a kid.'

Surprise lit up her eyes. 'Not good memories?'

He laced his fingers through hers, the need to touch her overwhelmingly strong. 'If a kid wants to come to a place like this then, like you say, it's going to be a great experience.'

'But not for you?'

He shook his head. 'I didn't want to be there and I resented that I had to go.' His fingers brushed the back of her hand, absorbing her softness. 'My younger sister, Sarah, had severe cerebral palsy. She'd been born at twenty-six weeks, was blind, severely contracted and needed twenty-four-hour care. I was five when she was born and I remember the hushed voices, the strained and grey faces of my parents and grandparents, and an overwhelming feeling that everything had just changed. It was weeks before she came home and when she did, she understandably absorbed my parents' time.'

'But at five you wouldn't have understood.' Kirby's keen eyes shone with empathy.

'No. As a kid I was consumed by a feeling that I had lost something huge but I didn't have the words to describe it. As Sarah got older and was permanently in a wheelchair, I realised she was never going to be any different and it was like a wound that never healed. Growing up I was both acutely embarrassed by Sarah and fiercely protective of her, especially if kids made crass remarks, but I just wanted to have a normal, healthy sister and be a normal kid. I craved a regular family, one where I could chase Sarah around the garden, tease her like a big brother is supposed to, and argue in the back seat during long car journeys.'

'And coming to camp just marked you as different.'

His head snapped up at the words that so aptly described what he'd been through. 'That's right. I always felt different. While my friends were off holidaying with their family or even getting to stay home and ride their bikes around the cul-de-sac, I was shunted off to camp.'

The vivid blue of her irises suddenly darkened. 'Or were you given the opportunity to have some freedom from your family?'

Her Pollyanna words gnawed at him, pulling at the child within. 'All I know is that had I ever been a father, I wouldn't be sending a kid to camp if he didn't want to go.'

'*Had* you ever been a father?' She leaned forward, her face earnest. 'You're thirty-three, with loads of time to become a father.'

He shook his head. 'Not after chemo, I don't. Chemotherapy doesn't differentiate between healthy cells and malignant ones, and it nukes sperm. One of the side effects is infertility.'

Her brows drew in, carving a deep V above her nose. 'I knew that. But surely you would have banked sperm before you started treatment?'

He folded his arms across his chest. 'I chose not to.'

'What?' Incredulity lay thick and heavy on the word. 'Why on earth would your doctors have allowed you to make that decision?'

'Allowed me?' Anger flashed inside him at her lack of understanding. 'I wasn't some naïve twenty-year-old, I was thirty-one and I knew what I wanted. I lived through my parents' unresolved grief after Sarah died so young and I saw the effect it had on their lives, felt the effect it had on my life. I want control over my life and I'm not taking any risks of having a disabled or sick child so a long time ago I made the decision that I didn't want to be a parent. Ever.'

Kirby abruptly pulled her hand out of his, her face flushing bright red and her eyes sparking with glints of pure rage. 'So you just tossed away a precious gift?'

Her fury rolled over him in ever-increasing waves, instantly putting him on the defensive. He stood up and walked around the table until he stood next to her. Drawing on every ounce of control he had, he managed to grind out a reply. 'Look, this was *my* choice and it has nothing at all to do with you.'

Her chest pushed in and out quickly, her breathing suddenly ragged. 'How could you?' Her voice rose, tinged with a maniacal edge, and her body shook. 'How could you give away your fertility, just like that, as if it was a disposable item?'

The thump of her fists on his chest caught him by surprise. He grabbed her wrists in self-defence, planning to set her back from him, but he caught a glimpse of her eyes and his breath left his lungs. Her raw grief knifed him, harrowing in its candour. What the hell was going on?

Kirby felt his vice-like grip against her skin and a surge of anguish poured through her. How could he have terminated his fertility? How could he have willingly given up the gift that had been stolen from her? Searing pain burned her chest, silver spots flickered against inky darkness and she heard a wrenching, guttural cry.

A moment later she became aware of soft-spun cotton cushioning her cheek and the reassuring pressure of Nick's arms holding her gently yet securely against him. His hands stroked her hair and his voice, low and mellow, caressed her ear. 'Breathe deeply, sweetheart, breathe, it will be OK.'

His calming voice, the tenderness of his arms and the heat

of his body soothed her, and her anger ebbed away. A tiny part of her tried to hold onto it but the flames had been doused as fast as they had flared, and the only thing left inside her was exhaustion. Exhaustion and embarrassment. How could she have lost control like that? She valued her control—it protected her.

But today it had gone AWOL and left her totally exposed. She sucked down a deep breath and buried her barrenness back where it belonged—out of sight but rarely out of mind. With superhuman effort she dragged her head up from Nick's sheltering shoulder and stepped out of his arms. She pushed her facial muscles up into a wan smile and levelled her gaze at his left ear.

'Please accept my sincere apologies.' She splayed her hands out in supplication. 'Sleep deprivation has obviously taken its toll on me but I promise you such an outburst won't ever happen again.' She turned toward the door. 'We better get back to the children.'

His hand caught hers, the grip firm. 'Kirby, two minutes ago you were hysterical. You're not ready to go back to the kids and right now they don't need you. Judy and Phillipa have everything under control and we can take a bit more time.' His keen gaze held hers, swirling with care and questions as his finger trailed down her cheek.

She tried to steel herself against the blissful sensations that coursed through every part of her. 'I'm just overtired.'

'There's more to it than that. I saw complete desolation in your eyes and I heard it in your voice. Tell me what's going on, I want to help.'

The empathy in his eyes, combined with the warmth of his touch, eroded her fragile façade and she closed her eyes for a moment, knowing that when she opened them she would have to tell him the whole truth.

She opened her eyes and strode to the freezer, hauling out two much-needed creamy vanilla ice creams covered in dark chocolate. If she had to bare her soul she needed comfort food. 'Here, catch.'

'Thanks.' Nick caught the confectionary, ripped open the gold foil wrapper, saluted her with the ice cream and then raised it to his lips, his mouth caressing the chocolate.

The memory of their kiss thundered through her and she bit down hard on her own ice cream, marshalling her thoughts. 'You can't help me but you do deserve an explanation, especially as I hit you, and I have *never* done that before to anyone in my life.' She gave a snort of derision. 'Not even to Anthony.'

He winked. 'Now, he might have deserved it.'

She managed a smile. 'You don't have to be this nice.'

He grinned at her—a look of pure magnetism. 'It's what I do.' He moved in next to her, his back against the freezer, his arm barely touching hers, and yet it pinned her with his support.

She bit her lip. 'I guess I start at the beginning. I met Anthony at a charity fundraiser for underprivileged children. He was ten years older than me, witty and entertaining, and he came from a large family, just like I did. We shared in common growing up in a chaotic household of kids, pets and love. He talked about how much he wanted to re-create those special times for children of his own and I knew exactly what he meant.'

A shudder ran through her. 'At least, I thought I did. Looking back, he actively chased me—flowers at work, helicopter rides to dinner and a whirlwind romance that culminated in his proposal three months later. He wanted to start a family straight away.'

Nick frowned. 'What about your career? Wouldn't waiting two years have been better for you?'

She dragged in a steadying breath, hating it that he could see so clearly what she had allowed to happen. 'Yes, but Anthony was nothing if not persuasive. He told me he was financially secure, and that he'd be a hands-on father and he'd support me to return to work to finish my training. I'd always seen children in my future so although it was all a bit faster than I wanted, I agreed that we'd start our family as soon as the ink was dry on the wedding certificate.'

'An old-fashioned honeymoon baby?'

She winced. 'Yep, but plans have a funny way of not working out. A few months before the wedding, in the middle of working flat out and trying to appease Anthony's mother, who wanted her son to have the full-catastrophe extravaganza, I missed two periods. I assumed I was pregnant and we were over the moon but…' She faltered, and took a bite of her ice cream, bracing herself for the words she really didn't want to speak.

'It's not unusual to skip a couple of periods during high-stress times.'

Nick's understanding voice encased her and she pushed on. 'If it had been that easy I wouldn't be standing here. When the blood-test report came back there were no signs of hCG.' She cleared her throat against the tightening sensation. 'I wasn't pregnant, my FSH levels were enormously high and my oestrogen was below the floor.'

'Premature ovarian failure.' He softly spoke the words for her as his hand slowly curled around hers. 'Are you sure it wasn't just a hormonal aberration?'

She shook her head. 'I prayed for that but I had a series of tests and for some reason my ovaries packed in at twenty-seven.'

'That totally sucks.' He rubbed his free hand through his hair, the silver strands on his temples glinting. 'So you and Anthony discussed adoption, right?'

She stared at him, her heart breaking. How was it that this man in front of her, this man who didn't want children of his own, could see that there was another path available? Her breath shuddered out as she spoke the final indignity. 'Anthony refused to discuss egg donors or adoption. He blamed me for causing the POF, blamed my workload, my focus on my career—blamed me, full stop. I went into shock, unable to believe his reaction, but that's when I realised…' She fisted her hands, willing herself to stay strong and steady.

Nick's frown deepened but his voice was gentle. 'That's when you realised what?'

She bit her lip. 'That he didn't love me. That I was just the means to his end.'

'I don't understand.' Clear green eyes bored into her, searching for an explanation.

'POF exposed the truth about my relationship, which it turns out was a sham. I had invested all my love in something that didn't exist.' She rubbed her forehead with her forefinger, trying to marshal her thoughts into a coherent sequence. 'Anthony was older than me and from a large Italian family. I had no idea that he'd been promised a huge amount of family money when he produced a grandchild. Apparently, when I met him, his business was struggling and he needed a cash injection so he'd borrowed against this promise of money.'

Nick's sharp intake of breath sounded in her ears but she pushed on, just wanting to get the story over with. 'It turns out that he'd come to the fundraiser with the express purpose of meeting someone who loved kids and would fall for his charm and happily provide him with the child he needed. I was the bunny that fell but the moment he found out I was faulty goods, he replaced me with Lisa, who, it appears, is as fertile as a rabbit.' She blinked rapidly, hating her own weakness. 'Their first child is due in a few months.'

'He's a complete bastard.'

She gave a watery laugh. 'Yeah, he is.'

'So really POF saved you.'

Startled, she looked up at him, not believing he had said those words. 'Saved me? It stole everything from me.'

He tilted his head, his brows raised in question. 'It saved you from a loveless marriage, and that has to be a good thing.'

She rolled his words through her brain, thinking about everything she'd lost, and with sudden clarity she realised she didn't have a single regret about losing Anthony. But she had a suitcase of regrets about her future. She was damaged goods. Most men wanted their own biological child and POF had stolen her chance to give any man that.

Not Nick.

She immediately discarded the thought, not wanting to go there. That was just heartache on a stick. She wanted kids in her future and her infertility burned inside her, hot and painful every time she thought about it. But she didn't want to talk about her infertility with Nick. He didn't want children, he'd actively chosen infertility and he wouldn't understand. No, they were at opposite ends of that spectrum with an almighty and unbreachable chasm between them.

She tossed her head and gave him a tight smile. 'Anyway, that's the past, it's over and I'm in Port, working with kids and getting my fill that way.'

He squeezed her hand, his expression earnest. 'You could do foster-care when you've finished your GP training.'

He was trying so hard to help, trying to make her feel better, and it tore shreds off her heart. Yes, she could do foster-care and it probably would be great, but it would also emphasise what she'd lost. Like most women, she wanted a man who loved her and a family, and she couldn't ever have that.

Tears threatened, pricking the backs of her eyes, and she couldn't stand there one more minute or she'd burst into tears or, worse, she'd throw herself back into his arms. Neither was a good idea and crying wasn't a good look, especially after she'd already had one emotional melt-down tonight. 'It's something to think about but right now I need to think about the four a.m. round and so do you.' She dropped her wooden ice-cream stick into the bin and regretfully but crucially pulled her hand out from under his. 'See you out there.'

Nick watched her walk through the door—head erect, shoulders straight and hips swaying. The sexiest walk he'd ever seen, and she didn't have a clue. *Faulty goods, my eye.* That lousy ex-fiancé had stolen her belief that she was a gorgeous and desirable woman and after all she'd been through the least she deserved was to get that back.

She needed to know that she was all woman, one hundred per cent deliciously hot, and he was just the man to show her. He smiled as anticipation shot through his veins. Planning this was going to be fun—executing it even better.

CHAPTER EIGHT

KIRBY checked her watch, stretched and smiled. Five to six on a Friday evening and time to head home. After the drama of the salmonella outbreak, the rest of the week had been blissfully tame medically speaking, with straightforward consultations and only one tourist coming to grief. He now had a white cast on his leg—a souvenir to remember Port by and a reminder of the night he'd over-indulged at the pub.

Somehow over the last few days she'd managed to regain her equilibrium and had done a reasonable job of faking an 'Aren't we good colleagues?' persona with Nick. She hated it that she'd completely broken down in front of him and she knew that because of that one emotional outburst he now thought of her differently. She'd caught him in the act of a sideways glance a few times—he was probably panicking she'd break down again and was counting the days until the summer was over and he could get back to Melbourne and more sane company.

He'd never mentioned their conversation again but she kept revisiting the pain on his face when he spoke about his sister. She chewed her lip and sighed. Everyone had their own share of heartache.

Just keep moving forward one step at a time.

She quickly scribbled down a list of jobs for Monday, including a phone call to Melinda's oncologist in Melbourne to get a treatment update. Then, gathering up her case histories and her bag, she headed out to Reception.

'Here you go, Vicki, all signed, notated and ready for you.' She dumped the folders onto the laminate counter.

'Thanks, dear.' Vicki's brown eyes bored into her from behind purple-framed glasses. 'So what have you got planned this evening?'

Kirby swallowed a sigh. Vicki asked her this question every Friday and never seemed satisfied with the answer. 'I'm picking up a new book from the newsagent's, grabbing a huge plate of seafood from the festival and then I'm going to sit on the deck, open a bottle of Barago merlot and watch the sunset over the ocean.'

And try not to think about Nick. Not think about how wonderful it had felt to be nestled against him, her head in the crook of his neck, his firm chest against hers… She pulled her attention back to Vicki, who had pursed her lips.

'Drinking alone, dear, that's not very wise.'

'But it's merlot so I can put the cork back in.' Kirby plastered on a smile and scooted to a safer topic. 'What are you doing this weekend?'

'My nephew, the lawyer from Melbourne—the one I was telling you about—arrived yesterday and is staying for a few days.' Vicki efficiently slotted the histories in the floor-to-ceiling filing cupboard.

'That will be fun for you, having a bit of company.' She knew how much Vicki missed her children.

The older woman nodded. 'Yes, but he won't want to

spend all his time with his old aunt.' A cunning smile twitched the corners of her mouth upward. 'I'm a bit weary tonight and I'd really appreciate it if you took him to the jazz-and-seafood festival.'

Kirby tried not to groan audibly. Vicki had been very good to her and she didn't want to hurt her feelings, but on the other hand she really didn't want to spend her Friday evening entertaining her nephew, no matter how rich and gorgeous he was purported to be. Her mind trawled for the right combination of words to gently reject the suggestion but the creak of the front door opening interrupted her. Nick strode in, radiating vibrant good health with a broad smile on his handsome face to match.

An increasingly familiar surge of undisguised need immediately flared deep inside her and her buttocks tightened instinctively. He looked good. More than good—bronzed, toned and holding a toolkit, he looked liked her fantasy.

A well-known surfing-brand T-shirt caressed his broad chest and crisply ironed stone-coloured shorts clad his muscular legs, but her eyes zeroed in on his wet hair, which she noticed now had enough length to curl at the nape of his neck. He looked fresh, clean and sun-kissed and she realised he must have recently stepped out of a shower. A vision of Nick naked slammed into her, drying her mouth.

Nick raised the red metal box in his hand. 'Vicki, I was on my way past and had my toolkit in the truck so I've fixed the wire door. It now closes properly and keeps the flies out, instead of inviting them into the waiting room.'

Vicki gave a cry of delight. 'Nick, you're wonderful. Talented *and* handy, and if I was thirty years younger, look out.'

Nick gave a deep rolling laugh, his eyes crinkling up with

the ease of a man comfortable in his own skin. 'You would have been far too much woman for me, Vicki.'

She chuckled. 'Well, that's right, I probably would have—I wore out Roger, bless him.' She started pressing the buttons on the security pad. 'So, Kirby, if you come with me now, I'll introduce you to Andrew.'

Kirby thought she saw a ripple of tension cross Nick's shoulders but she didn't have time to wonder about that and it was probably just his muscles countering the weight of the toolbox. She *so* didn't want to spend the evening with Andrew and desperate situations meant desperate measures.

Ignoring every lesson she'd learned at her mother's knee, she prepared herself to lie. She'd make something up about a clinic problem and she fervently hoped Nick would just roll with it and not question her in front of Vicki. She'd apologise and explain it all to him later, after Vicki had left and she was off the hook from dating Andrew. 'I'm really sorry, Vicki, but Nick didn't just come to fix the wire door. I asked him to come in because—'

'The fact is, Vicki, she wants me, not Andrew.' Nick winked, his eyes sparkling with pure devilment. 'She's taking *me* to the festival.'

Kirby almost choked on the spot. His audacity was unbelievable and a barrage of indignant words poured into her mouth, preparing to unleash her wrath. But they immediately clagged against her tongue as she realised none of them could be spoken without giving her away. Her lie neatly corralled every word, leaving her completely exposed and at its mercy. At Nick's mercy. What was he playing at?

Vicki's grin almost split her face and she gave Kirby a knowing look, one that said, *You're a sly one but he's as sexy as hell, so of course you want him.* 'Why didn't you just say that you and Nick are an item instead of hiding behind that silly story about drinking alone?'

Oh, great, now she looked like a desperate alcoholic. 'I—'

Nick slipped his free arm through Kirby's, his fingers firmly entwining with hers. He tilted his head, giving Vicki a serious look. 'We wanted to keep it quiet. You know what Port's like.'

Kirby could feel his body vibrating with suppressed laughter and it took every ounce of control not to kick him. Although Vicki could keep patient confidentiality, when it came to relationships, she was Port's biggest gossip. The moment her foot hit the outside step, this bit of news would roar through the town faster than a cyclone.

'Absolutely, Nick, I understand completely.' Vicki crossed the waiting room with a firm and decisive step and turned just as she reached the door. Tapping her nose with her forefinger, she beamed at them. 'You two have a lovely time. Your secret is safe with me.'

The moment the door banged shut Nick's hand tightened on Kirby's. 'Come on, we better get to this festival.' A wolfish grin moved across his face. 'After all, the entire town will be expecting us.'

She stared up at him, drawn by the look in his eye—laughter mixed with a simmering charisma. She should be furious with him, she should be vibrating with indignation at his highhandedness and she should be saying, *No, I'm not coming to the festival with you.* Instead, she followed him out the door, her brain stuck fast on the fact that the entire town would be assuming she was having sex with Nick Dennison while her body ached on the fact that she wasn't.

* * *

The mellow sound of a saxophone drifted across the air and Kirby fell back on the picnic rug. 'I couldn't eat another thing.'

'I'm surprised you managed that last plate of calamari.' Nick grinned as he leaned over her, sipping his wine. 'It's wonderful to see a woman with a healthy appetite, although more of my veggies wouldn't hurt.'

She gazed up him, taking in the way his thick chocolate-brown lashes brushed his cheeks, how his stubble creased along deep smile lines that converged into dimples, and how much younger he looked than he had a few weeks ago when she'd first met him. The last vestiges of his treatment had completely faded, leaving him more handsome than any man deserved to be.

He'd been attentive all evening in a casual way—slinging his arm across her shoulders as they'd wandered from stall to stall, feeding her samples of everything from prawns to oysters, and choosing the perfect local sauvignon blanc to match the delicious food. He'd made a point of holding her hand when they'd met the self-obsessed Andrew, and he'd teased her on and off all evening that she owed him big time for saving her from an evening of boredom.

Now he put his glass down and grabbed her hand. 'Come on, you'll feel better if you move.'

'I don't believe you.' She groaned as she let him pull her to her feet, enjoying the way his other arm snaked around her waist, holding her close.

'I wouldn't lie to you.' His eyes danced as he lowered his head and his voice rumbled against her ear. 'And I promise you, I'll make it worthwhile.'

Shimmering tingles raced from her head to her toes, streaking through her like wildfire and igniting everything in its wake until she quivered and she felt sure he would feel it.

'Hello, Doctors, lovely evening for it.'

She looked up through dazed eyes to see Doug Reardon tipping his hat as he walked past arm in arm with his wife.

Nick laughed and waved. 'A perfect evening for it.' He turned back to face her, shooting her a deadpan look. 'It's a funny thing but the whole town has been giving us indulgent looks all night.'

She rolled her eyes. 'I can't imagine why.' She broke away from him and started to walk, needing to move, driven by a need to leave the crowded foreshore park and get away from those knowing looks—looks that inferred something that didn't exist and never would. She headed out along the pier road, suddenly desperate to be home.

Nick fell easily into step with her. 'They like to see a couple in love.'

She increased her pace. 'We're not in love.'

'No, we're not.'

His words relaxed her. They weren't in love and the fact they both wanted totally different things out of life made them almost incompatible, but they laughed together and they were friends. *Think friendship.* A crazy laugh bounced around her head.

He stepped in closer so his arm touched hers and his heat soared through her. 'But we are in lust.'

His husky voice filled with desire brought her to an abrupt halt. She swung around to face him, her hands gripping her hips as she desperately tried to keep some distance. 'Speak for yourself.'

'I am.' His eyes, shaded by the fading light, flared with unconcealed desire. 'You're the sexiest woman I've met in a long time.'

Her heart hammered hard and fast as his sweet words rolled over her like honey. But she couldn't listen to them—she'd learned that words counted for little and these ones had heartache written all over them. 'You don't get out very often, do you?'

'I get out plenty.' He trailed his finger down her cheek. 'You're gorgeous, you're sexy and you're driving me crazy.'

She wanted to slam her hands against her ears to drown out his beguiling voice. 'This is crazy. We're colleagues, we want different things.' She started walking again with no clear direction, just letting her feet take her as her body buzzed with need and her brain raced with incoherent thoughts that tumbled chaotically over each other.

He quickly caught up with her, his voice insistent. 'Pretending we're just colleagues and friends is the crazy part. You want me as much as I want you.'

She strode along the road, hating it that she did want him so badly. Hating that he knew. Folding her arms across her chest, she forced herself to be the sensible one. 'I didn't know conceit was a tool of seduction. Is that how you've always got women to jump into bed with you?'

His hand touched her sleeve, his expression suddenly serious and his mouth curving into a wry smile. 'I've never had to try this hard with any woman. You've reduced me to begging.'

She stared at him in amazement. Raw need rolled off him, almost toppling her with its intensity. Deep inside her something cracked and she steeled herself against a crumbling sensation. 'It won't work.' But her voice sounded unconvincing.

Surprise streaked across his handsome face as if the thought had never occurred to him. 'Of course it will.'

'No, it won't.' She shook her head, trying to hold onto the

last shreds of her resistance and common sense. 'You have your carefree childless life all mapped out, and that's the opposite of what I want.'

'You're over-thinking this.' He ran his hands down her arms, a touch gentle yet packing a seismic punch. 'This isn't for ever, this is all about now. It doesn't have to be complicated—in fact, it's pretty simple. I want you, you want me. It's summer, the season of being carefree, and we're both here for the summer so let's use this time we have together, use it for fun.'

His hand cupped her jaw, his expression suddenly earnest. 'Hell, both of us deserve some carefree fun after what we've been through. Let's wind the clock back to real carefree times and pretend we're sixteen.'

This is all about now. Tempting images bombarded her, collapsing all her worries about her future into a locked box. 'I was a very organised and responsible sixteen.'

His mouth curved up into a long, slow, seductive smile and his eyes twinkled. 'Then this is your chance to reinvent yourself.'

Reinvent herself? The thought tumbled through her, over and over, gathering massive appeal. She'd always been thoughtful, conscientious, a planner, and where had that left her? Shattered and alone. She was tired of worrying about what came next in her life so perhaps it was time to try something new, something just for her, just for a short time. Real life would intrude soon enough and knowing that they wanted such different things would protect her. Yes, this would be fun.

Bad idea. Very bad idea.

She instantly argued—no, it wasn't. Hell, the whole town thought they'd been at it like rabbits so why not do what was already considered a done deal? Standing strong against the constant barrage of need that burned inside her had worn her to a frazzle. Nick was right, she did want him. She wanted him so badly she throbbed with emptiness. This was her chance to reinvent herself, take something for herself. 'No plans, no future, just the summer?'

'No plans, no future, just the summer.' Nick held his breath, watching the war of emotions on Kirby's face. From the moment he'd capitalised on her lie earlier and set her up in the clinic, the entire evening had been a gamble—exciting, enjoyable and totally unpredictable. He'd loved every minute of it and now it all came down to this moment.

Silently, Kirby stepped forward, looped her arms around his neck, tilted her head up and seared his lips with a kiss of pure hunger, devoid of any restraint.

Yes! Hot, firm and fast, the kiss thundered through him, and he instantly hardened while his head spun. His arms moved to pull her tightly against him but as abruptly as she'd kissed him she stepped away, turned and ran down the empty pier.

'Hey! That's not playing fair.'

Her laughter came back to him on the evening breeze. With sheer strength of will he managed to force enough blood back to his limbs so he could walk down the pier. As he got closer, the yellow light of the rising moon illuminated her hair, giving her a golden halo. An angel with a body for sin.

She threw him a crooked smile. 'What kept you?' Grabbing his hand, she quickly started jogging down the pier steps toward the moored boats.

A moment ago with the smugness of experience he'd thought he had her, but now he wasn't quite so sure. Somehow he'd lost control of the situation and now his planned seduction was unravelling in front of him. Nothing about Kirby was predictable. 'Where are you going?'

She didn't reply but kept walking, her feet slapping against the boards of the lower pier. Dropping his hand, she hauled hard on a rope and then jumped down onto the deck of a yacht, its sleek white bow glowing against the dark water. She shot him a smile loaded with the promise of all good things. 'You said you wanted sixteen, so that's what I'm giving you.'

The fantasy hit him so hard he nearly lost his balance and pitched into the water. Staring down at her, he concentrated hard and managed to force out the words. 'I said carefree, not breaking the law. Are you allowed on this boat?'

She stared straight back at him, blue eyes swirling with a wildness he'd never seen before. Keeping her gaze fixed with his, she crossed her arms across her chest and hooked her fingers around the base of her T-shirt. Very slowly, she drew the clingy Lycra over her head and let it trail through her fingers until it fell to the deck.

The sonorous sound of a double bass and clarinet combo, carried by the breeze, and the steady slap of the water against the boat instantly faded as his brain emptied and every sense zeroed in on creamy white breasts nestled against a black lace bra. His pants felt tight.

She tossed her head back, the action full of sass as a curtain of hair swirled around her face and brushed her shoulders. 'So, are you coming?'

Probably. Letting go of every cautious thought, every shred of common sense, he jumped down onto the deck as Kirby disappeared through the hatch and into the cabin.

He found her skirt on the third step as he stumbled into the tiny space. 'Don't you dare go any further without me.' The words came out on a growl loaded with sexual frustration.

Laughing, she lay down on the tiny bed, a vixen smile on her face as she bent her knees and crossed her long legs, twirling one ankle at him. 'Well, hurry up, then.'

Somehow he managed to shuck his pants in the tiny space without banging his head. He lowered himself onto the mattress, supporting himself on his left elbow, his right hand trailing through her hair. 'A good lover is never rushed.'

'Is that so?' She raised her hand to his cheek. 'I've never met a good sixteen-year-old lover—they tend to be fumbling fingers, expired condoms, all talk, and mighty quick on the main event.'

He stilled, realising he wasn't as prepared as he'd thought. He'd planned to seduce her at his house. 'I don't have a condom.'

She bit her lip, the fun in her eyes instantly dimming. 'Neither of us really needs one, do we?'

Her bleak look pierced him—it didn't belong in their fantasy and the need to banish it consumed him. He traced the line of her jaw with his finger, savouring her softness and breathing in her jumbled scent of wildflowers and salt. 'Then we have the perfect fantasy, don't we? A stolen space and no contraception, but there is going to be one very big difference.'

'What's that?' Huge blue eyes absorbed him.

'The main event is going to take all night.'

The moment his mouth touched hers, Kirby gave herself up to him. Nothing existed except Nick—the pressure of his mouth, the graze of his stubble, his taste of salt and wine, and the scorching touch of his body against hers.

His deep kiss penetrated way beyond her mouth, his tongue eliciting a surge of response from every cell between her lips and her toes. And when he'd kissed her to the point where her mind had completely melted, he trailed kisses along her jaw, across the hollow of her throat and down to the lace of her bra. She was vaguely aware of his right hand under her back and a moment later her bra fastening was released, the cups falling away and her breasts spilling out.

She gazed into emerald eyes. 'You've done that before.'

A sheepish look crossed his face. 'I learned that technique at sixteen.'

But her quip morphed into a moan of bliss as his mouth closed over her breast, his tongue tracing her nipple, drawing it up into a hot, hard peak and sending spirals of white light thudding through her.

He lifted his head and grinned. 'I learned this technique a bit later.'

She caught her breath. 'I think you've refined it.'

He lowered his head again, this time paying close attention to her other breast. Exquisite shafts of tingling sensation—half pleasure, half pain—shot from her breast to a single point deep inside her. Gripping his back, she gasped in delight as her hips rose instinctively up toward him, needing to feel him hard against her.

His wicked laugh rained down on her. 'If you like that, then you might enjoy this.' His lips started to press hot kisses down her belly.

Every part of her craved to lie back and let him give her what she knew would be beyond wonderful, but instead she grabbed his head to stop him, sinking her hands into his hair.

'Problem?' He raised his head, a questioning expression clinging to his cheeks.

'Big problem.' She'd fantasised about running her hands

through his hair, pressing her palms against his smooth chest and exploring him in the same way he was exploring her, but if she let him continue, she'd miss her chance. Somehow she managed to get her liquid muscles to function and she wriggled out from under him, pushing at his right shoulder and laughing at the confused look on his face.

He rolled over onto his back, bringing her with him. 'I thought you would have enjoyed that.'

Straddling him, she leaned forward, her hair caressing his face. 'I would have adored it and I'm only taking a short rain-check.' She leaned back, her fingers flicking up the base of his T-shirt, pushing it up his chest, before pulling it over his head. Golden skin, taut abdominal muscles and a trail of dark hair that knifed downward from his navel assaulted her gaze and she sighed. 'You once told me I'd enjoy this sight. I hate it when you're right.'

The rich green of his eyes darkened. 'Gaze all you want, I'm yours for the night.'

Yours for the night. She hugged the words close. 'I'm done gazing.' She reached out, splaying her fingers over his heart and feeling the fast beat vibrating underneath her hands. A heart beating wildly and matching her own erratic rhythm—one of blissful anticipation mixed with unfulfilled need. 'I've wanted to touch you like this from the moment I met you.' Tracing his pectoral muscles, her fingers roved over the small patch of thickened skin—scar tissue from his treatment and the only flaw on a perfect landscape. Then she dipped and curved until she circled his nipple, tweaking it gently between her fingers.

His pupils dilated and his thighs stiffened underneath her. She laughed, loving it that she could get such a response from him.

With a feather-light touch she continued downward, outlining the sinew and tendon of the solid pack of muscles and then trailing down to outline and cup the straining fabric of his jocks.

He bucked underneath her as a low growl left his throat. 'It's been a long time, Kirby, so if you don't want real sixteen…'

Her fingers caressed as she hooked his gaze. 'Can't you handle the heat?'

Challenge flared in his eyes and he immediately slid his hand down between them, sliding a finger firmly along the crotch of her panties.

Sensation exploded and her breath came hard and fast. She lost all focus on him, her body pushing hard against his hand, needing to rise on the surge of ecstasy that fireballed through her, leaving every part of her begging for more. 'Don't stop.'

'Sweetheart, I've hardly started.'

He flipped her over onto her back and using his mouth and hands he fuelled her already ragged need until every muscle deep inside her quivered, desperate to tense against hard flesh. She was past flirting, past banter, past pretence. She didn't care about anything except the driving need to have him deep inside her. 'Nick.' She almost sobbed his name. 'Now.'

Nick stared down at Kirby, her hair spread out on the bed, her eyes large and wide in her flushed face, and he didn't think he'd ever seen anything so beautiful. It had been so long since he'd been with a woman and she was driving him past control, but he wanted to give her this, she deserved it. 'Just enjoy, this one's for you.'

Her fingers sank into his shoulders with an iron grip and her eyes, wild with hunger, fixed with his. 'No, this one's for us.'

He'd dreamed about this moment for weeks. He slid into

her with ease, as if he belonged there. She rose up to meet him, capturing him deeply, stroking him as he stroked her and they rose together as one, flinging themselves out to the stars, beyond the pull of reality.

CHAPTER NINE

NICK stood in waist-deep water, his back fiery hot from the sun, in total contrast to his belly where occasional trickles of icy Southern Ocean water chilled his skin, having penetrated his thick, black wetsuit. White, briny foam buffeted him and the sand under his feet moved as the tail end of each wave raced past him to the shore.

'Now!' Nick cupped his hands around his mouth like a megaphone, trying to make himself heard over the surf. 'Stand up now, Cameron.'

The determined twelve-year-old gripped the side of his board and launched himself from his knees for the fourteenth time in a row, his feet swinging forward to stand against the lumps of wax that roughened the surfboard. He stood, he wobbled, and he fell as the board soared skywards before slamming back down onto the waves, brought to earth by the black cord attached to the ankle strap. A moment later Cameron's head appeared above the waves, water streaming across his face.

'Do you want to take a break?' Nick motioned to the boy who'd been at it for half an hour.

'No.' Cameron shook his head and doggedly clambered back on the surfboard and paddled back out to try again.

Splashes of cold water unexpectedly hit Nick's back and he turned to find a laughing Kirby, body board hooked under one arm, scooping water and tossing it at him with the other. Her eyes sparkled vivid blue, matching the ocean, her face glowed with vitality and her full-length wetsuit clung skin-tight, outlining every sensual curve. Despite the icy water, his body instantly responded. Like it did every time he saw her.

Still splashing him, she continued moving forward until she stood next to him, her cinnamon-apple scent circling him, taking him instantly back to last night when he'd buried his face in her hair. *Buried yourself deep inside her.*

He splashed her back, laughter rocking through him at her joyful shrieks. A week had passed since the festival, a week of fun, hard work and the most amazing sex of his life. He felt alive in a way he'd never known before, different even from his life prior to getting sick. Colours were brighter, sounds more complex and his energy for work and his energy for Kirby bounded out of him.

She wrapped the body board's Velcro strap around her wrist, her expression filled with curiosity. 'I didn't expect to see you down here—I thought you said you had capsicums to pick.'

He gave a wry smile. 'I do, but when I called by KC the unit C boys cornered me and asked if I'd teach them how to surf.' He swung his arm in an arc. 'Today's conditions are perfect.'

'You called by KC?' Incredulity clung to the words, matching the surprised expression on her face.

He nodded stiffly. 'Judy asked me to talk to one of the boys.'

Her eyes widened. 'And you said yes?'

'Judy can be very persuasive.' A ripple of irritation mixed with discomfiture wove through him. He didn't want to examine too closely why he'd deliberately not mentioned

Judy's call to Kirby, but the disbelief on her face that he'd got involved at KC unexpectedly morphed his irritation into a jag of indignation.

He tried to shrug it off because, if the truth be known, he'd been just as surprised as Kirby at the 'yes' that had slipped out of his mouth when Cameron had asked him to stay and help with surfing.

Two boys shot passed them, riding their boards expertly into the shallows.

'Great going, guys.' Nick raised his arms to shoulder height and held out both his thumbs above two closed fists.

Grinning widely, the two boys waved back before running back out toward the breakers, ready to try again.

'They're going really well. Perhaps I should ask you to teach me because I can never manage to get up off my stomach.'

'Ben and Steven are naturals.'

She threw him an arch look. 'And you're saying I'm not?'

He wasn't falling for that one. He moved his head close to her and whispered, 'You're amazing, beautiful and you have skills and talents in other areas.'

Her face flushed and he laughed at her blush. 'After last night I didn't think anything would embarrass you.'

She tossed her head, her plump lips forming into a pout. 'You're totally wicked, mentioning *that* in daylight.' She turned away but a smile lingered on her lips as she stared out toward the horizon.

Nick longed to pull her into his arms and kiss her until her breath was ragged and she collapsed hard against him. But he was on duty and he could already predict the reaction he'd get from the group of pubescent boys if he kissed her, which would range from 'Oh, yuck' through to jeering sniggers.

'How's Cam doing?' Kirby pointed to the red-headed boy in the group of other wannabe surfers from KC.

'He's determined, I'll give him that, and he's almost got there a few times. He just has to find his centre and go with the movement rather than fighting it.' He cupped his hands again and yelled, 'Try this one, mate.'

She elbowed him gently in the ribs. 'You've got a bit of a soft spot for him, haven't you? That's why you're here.'

He bristled against her words. 'No, I'm here because seven boys tackled me to the ground and refused to get off me until I said yes.'

She rolled her eyes. 'Yeah, right. Come on, why not just admit it? You like the kid.'

He felt a muscle in his jaw twitch. 'No more than any of the other kids.'

'Yes, more than any of the other kids. During the salmonella outbreak and in the post-recovery check-ups I saw you taking a special interest in Cameron.'

He should have known nothing got past Sherlock, she noticed everything. In the last two weeks he'd recognised a lot of his twelve-year-old self in Cameron, but he didn't want to talk about it. Avoiding her gaze, he tried to sound offhand. 'He's had a tough year with his diagnosis of diabetes.'

Kirby tilted her head, as her eyebrows rose. '*And* his younger brother is severely autistic. I saw him in full flight the day Cameron arrived and it was pretty distressing for everyone.'

He let her words hang on the salt-tinged breeze, not wanting to acknowledge that he understood some of the stuff Cam was facing. Not wanting to risk getting close to the guilt that hovered around his heart whenever he thought of Sarah and how he'd lost her just when he'd been old enough to really understand.

Her free hand touched his shoulder. 'I think it's wonderful that you can help each other.'

Her words rained down on him, exacerbating the already swirling emotions that pulled at his gut, but it was anger that emerged from the melee. Hell, he didn't need any help! 'It's a surfing lesson, Kirby, that's all. It's a way of spending time before I return to Melbourne Central.' He shrugged off her hand, shrugged off her inference and waded out a bit further, shouting to Cameron. 'You can do this. Hands forward, knees in the middle of the board, paddle, paddle, now up!'

The boy planted his left leg forward and with a very wobbly stance rose up with his arms outstretched. The board nudged forward on the crest of the wave and scooted down the curve with Cam standing tall and proud.

Thirty seconds later the wave collapsed completely and Cam fell off, victorious. 'I did it, Nick, I did it!'

Nick slapped his palm against the boy's, an overwhelming sense of triumph fizzing in his veins. 'That was awesome. I'm really proud of you.'

Cam flicked water from his eyes, his achievement suddenly dimming on his face. 'I wish Dad could have seen me.'

The wistful words kicked Nick hard in the gut. He remembered those moments when his own father had been caught up with the care of Sarah and had missed out on seeing his successes. As an adult he knew his father must have hated the choices he'd had to make but as a kid Nick had never understood. It was yet another reason why he was never going to be a father.

He clapped his hand onto Cam's shoulder. 'I know, mate, but by Parents' Day next week you'll be a pro and you can show your dad then.' He hoped the weather co-operated and that Cam's dad could actually make it.

* * *

'Can you lift it a bit higher?' Kirby called to Nick, who stood high on a ladder.

'Like this?' His strong arms swung the large rope around one of KC's imposing brick gateposts.

Kirby clapped her approval, childlike excitement flicking through her. 'Perfect.'

Leaning sideways, his tanned legs locked in a solid stance and his muscular back taut with tension, he tied the KC banner in place so it hung high over the entrance.

With his back to her, Kirby took the chance to openly stare at him. It didn't matter that she knew every part of his body in intimate detail, she never tired of gazing at him, watching and loving the way his work-hardened body moved—poetry in motion.

The light morning sea breeze fluttered the red, blue and white bunting as a flock of fifteen pelicans flew overhead, their enormous wings slicing through the air with stately grace, as if giving their approval to the events below. Nick moved quickly down the ladder and walked over to Kirby, his face creased in a wide and mischievous grin. 'I now declare the annual Kids' Cottage fete open.'

She laughed. 'I think perhaps the celebrity patron does that in a couple of hours.'

'That'd be right. I do all the hard work and that other bloke gets the glory.' His grumbling tone was at odds with his twinkling eyes.

She stepped up to him, wrapping her arms around his waist. 'Are you feeling under-appreciated?'

He dropped his forehead down to touch hers. 'Well, I did risk life and limb at the top of that ladder.'

'So you did.' She brushed away a curl of his hair that had

fallen across his eyes, loving that it was now long enough that she could do that. Leaning in, she pressed her lips to his, her mouth so familiar against his that it zeroed straight to the place that always made him shudder against her. She looked up and grinned. 'Feeling more valued?'

His eyes, sparkling in myriad hues of green, glinted back at her. 'Almost, but I'm sure I can take some more thanking tonight after this shindig is over.'

She loved teasing him. 'It's going to be a huge day and I'm sure you'll be way too exhausted.'

'Never.'

The word rolled out low and guttural, loaded with energy that swirled around her, pulling her in.

'Well, I might be. By the time I've done my time on the face-painting stall, read two books in the story-time tent and staffed the first-aid tent, I'll be ready for a long soak in the spa and a foot rub.'

A long, lazy smile moved into his cheeks, carving out swirling dimples. 'I'm sure that can be arranged. But meanwhile to keep your strength up and to make sure you actually stop for lunch, how about we meet at twelve o'clock at the barbeque tent? We'll both be ready for a hamburger by then.'

Warmth flowed through her at the suggestion. 'I'll be there. But what are you up to for the next few hours?'

He winked at her. 'It's a top-secret mission and I'd have to kill you if I told you so don't ask.' He then kissed her on the bridge of her nose and with a backwards wave walked off with his ladder.

She stood watching his retreating back, unable to keep a huge smile from her face despite the fact she was completely confounded by his caginess about what he was doing with his morning. He had moments of being deliberately vague and she suddenly realised it always happened when it involved the kids.

Just like with Cam and the surfing. He'd been great with Cam but whenever she tried to talk to him about it he sent up a towering brick wall between them and clammed up completely or changed the subject. She didn't get it. He obviously enjoyed the things he was doing at KC and was becoming increasingly involved with the children—he'd even arranged for someone else to man his Saturday market stall today and offered his help to Judy to be part of the biggest fundraising event on the KC calendar.

The annual fete was huge. All the favourite drawcards were in place—the giant jumpy castle and a calliope playing carousel for the pre-schoolers, the stomach-churning Rota and dodgem cars for the teenagers, the enormously high and long slide and a petting zoo for kids of all ages. Then there were the rows of white marquees, starting with the white elephant stall where one person's trash was immediately converted to another person's treasure. The handicraft stall was the domain of the Ladies' Auxiliary, where a year's worth of production was on display from lovingly knitted football teddies to layers of brightly coloured tulle used to create dolls, the ardent wish of every little girl's heart.

Kirby was never certain which stall was her favourite—the cake stall, with its fluffy cream-filled sponge cakes with passionfruit icing, home-made buttery shortbread in clear cellophane bags tied with gold curling ribbon, and deep-red raspberry preserves, or the quiet retreat of the Devonshire Tea tent, with hot tea, hot scones and lashings of Port Bathurst cream straight from the farm.

She quickly walked past a clown who was surrounded by

a circle of fascinated children intently watching his hands quickly sculpt long thin balloons into animal shapes, and she took her place at the face-painting table. The crowd was building as every good fete attendee knew the tip was to get in early to get top pick of all the stock and be back at the beach by the time the sun got really hot.

Kirby angled the large market umbrella so it cast a large circle of shade over her and her customers, tied an apron over herself to protect her clothes from the paint and displayed her designs.

'I'd like to be a tiger, please.' An eight-year old girl with a helium balloon tied to her wrist held out her coin.

'One tiger coming up.' Kirby dipped her brush into the yellow and set to work, loving the delight on the kids' faces when she showed them their new look in the mirror.

The morning streaked past in a blur of faces, conversations and storytelling and by eleven-thirty Kirby had finished her morning's duties and was starving. With half an hour before she had to meet Nick she jammed her sunhat onto her head, bought a fruit smoothie and took the chance of exploring the fete before her afternoon duty in the first-aid centre started. Teenagers congregated around the stage, enjoying the Battle of the Bands, which was in full swing, and further over children cuddled in their parents' laps, squealing with delight as they raced down the bumpy slides.

That should have been me. Kirby sipped her drink against the lump that formed in her throat, trying to push the hollow feeling that pervaded her every time she saw families together. Looking for distraction, she headed toward the noisiest queue of shrieking and laughing children and as she got closer she realised most of the kids were KC campers who got to enjoy the fete too.

A form of scaffolding with a swing seat had been erected in the centre of a pool of water with a large painted target fixed behind it. The banner above declared, 'Dunk the Doctor' and Nick, wearing boardies, a rash top and a lifesaving cap, sat high in the chair.

Kirby blinked, unable to believe her eyes. The doctor who'd been so adamant a few weeks ago that he was not working with children had put himself up as a sideshow attraction. By the look on his face, he was loving every minute of it.

First there had been his work with Cameron and now this. Her heart soared. They were having the best summer and he no longer held himself back from children. Perhaps what they both wanted had drawn closer together. Suddenly a daydream floated through her mind of Nick and herself surrounded by children. Adopted children.

Be careful, no plans—remember.

But she ignored the voice. Nick was nothing like Anthony. She and Nick shared a million things in common, including great sex and laughter.

She returned Nick's big wave to her and the huge teasing smile on his face, watching him as he leaned forward and called to the kid at the front of the line. 'I'm getting hot up here.'

'Do your best, Cameron,' Kirby called out. 'Take him out.'

Cameron grinned, straightened his shoulders and hefted the basketball he was holding above his head, aiming for the big black circle.

The crowd chanted, 'One, two, three.'

Cam threw the ball, putting his entire twelve-year-old

effort behind it. It hit the target with accuracy, the chair tipped backwards and Nick somersaulted into the water with a satisfying splash.

The crowd roared, Cameron stood taller and Kirby laughed so hard her ribs ached.

A sopping wet Nick surfaced, water streaming off his handsome face, and he climbed out of the pool, immediately clapping Cam on the shoulder. 'Great throw, mate. Now go and get yourself a prize from Mrs Dalton.'

A glow of success emanated from the boy. 'Thanks, Doc. That was awesome!'

Cameron ran off and Kirby handed Nick a towel. 'I wish I'd known. I would have been here earlier with my camera.'

He slung the towel around his neck and gave her a wicked grin loaded with mischief. 'The local paper beat you to it. I'm next week's centrefold.'

Kirby shook her head in smiling bemusement. 'Is there any room next to that giant ego for me to walk beside you?'

'For you—' he put on a fake Italian accent '—always. But so you can walk close I'll just get changed out of this wet gear.'

'Meet me in the food line.' Kirby followed the aroma of barbecued onions and joined the meandering line, enjoying chatting to Jake, Gaz and Meryl while she waited, still stunned that Nick had got so involved in the fete. *He's got involved with the children.*

She'd just paid for the burgers when he arrived by her side, all tousled hair and glowing good health. She held out the ubiquitous white bag with the two twisted ears. 'Yours has the lot, including pineapple and beetroot.'

'Sweet.' He ripped open the bag and took a big bite from the burger.

'Hungry, are you?' Smiling, Kirby pulled some stray onion out of her bun and nibbled on it.

He pretended to be affronted. 'You try being knocked into the water fifteen times. It generates an appetite.'

They sat at a table in the shade of a grove of gnarled tea trees and Kirby neatly pulled open her white bag, dividing it down the seam line to make a mat for her hamburger. Nick had almost finished his and was eyeing hers when the music on the loudspeaker stopped and Judy's voice came on instead.

'Could Dr Atherton or Dr Dennison please come to the sick bay *now*.'

'Must be something more than a cold pack or a plaster can fix or Phillipa would have dealt with it.' Kirby stood up and started walking.

Nick picked up her burger and handed it to her. 'Eat and run. We don't need you getting sick too.'

They jogged to the sick bay. Jordan, one of the unit C boys, sat in the chair, his face alabaster white underneath a large trickling bloodstain. Phillipa had a gauze-covered ice pack on his head and looked up with relief as they walked in.

Kirby stepped up to the boy who looked so little and immediately felt for him, knowing he probably wanted his mother. 'Jordan, you poor—'

But he looked past her, straight to Nick.

'Mate, what have you done to yourself?' Nick immediately pulled on a pair of gloves and lifted up the ice pack.

'I ran into a pole.'

'Jumped out at you, did it?' Kirby opened up some saline, feeling slightly ignored. 'I think unit C is going to win the camp award for most admissions to the sick bay.'

'You wouldn't have let Ben run off with your prize, would

you, Dr Nick?' Jordan shot Nick a conspiratorial look that clearly said, *A girl wouldn't understand.*

'No way. I would have chased him down as well.' He bobbed down in front of the boy and shone a torch into Jordan's black hair. 'But you hit that pole so hard you've split the skin.'

'Skin glue?' Phillipa opened the medical kit, her fingers hovering over the tray.

Nick shook his head. 'It starts on his forehead but extends into his hairline so it's going to have to be stitches.'

'No way.' Jordan's eyes welled up.

Nick squeezed his shoulder. 'You'll have a manly scar and a good story to match it. I've got a few of those.'

'Have you?' Watery curiosity shone in Jordan's eyes.

'Yep. See this one?' He pointed to a faint line on his forearm. 'I fell off the top of the brick fence when I was trying to be Superman. I also broke my leg.'

'Did you have crutches and a cast?'

'I did.'

'Cool!' Admiration shone in the boy's eyes before dimming slightly. 'But I won't need crutches.'

'No, but you'll have a bit of a pirate scar, which is mysterious.'

Needing something to do now she'd finished her hamburger, Kirby drew up the local anaesthetic and handed it to Nick, who chatted away to Jordan about the current test cricket match, as if they were walking down to the beach for a surf instead of injecting lignocaine into his scalp in preparation for suturing. She watched him bring the skin edges together with tiny stitches, his brow furrowed in serious concentration, yet all the time trading sporting statistics to keep Jordan relaxed.

Deep inside her something ached—this was the man who so unalterably believed he didn't want to be a father. Couldn't he see he'd be great?

He snipped the black nylon, separating it from the final stitch, and dropped the needle into the suture tray. 'Phillipa will put a dressing on that and you won't be able to wash your hair for five days, which probably won't be too much of a hardship given your allergy to shower water.' Humour played through his words while the sound of latex snapped sharply as he stripped off his gloves and dropped them in the bin. 'You have to stay in sick bay for the rest of the day due to the bump on your head.'

Jordan slumped. 'But I'll miss the rest of the fete.'

'Yes, but you'll get ice cream and jelly and a personal visit from the celebrity patron.' Nick helped Jordan up onto the bed. 'He's a pretty famous runner and he might just autograph your camp book if you ask him politely.'

The boy settled back into the pillows slightly more happy. 'That would be great but can *you* come see me again later?'

Kirby caught the longing in the boy's voice. First Cameron and now Jordan. Nick had an easy way with these boys that generated respect and admiration.

Nick nodded. 'No problem. I'll drop by before I go home and I'll ring your mum and tell her what happened and that you're OK. Catch you later.' He gave the lad a playful punch before crossing the room.

'Here you go, Jordan.' Phillipa bustled about with gauze and tape.

Nick caught Kirby's arm and propelled her through the door. 'Come on, I'll buy you some tea and scones, I know they're your favourite.'

'Bye, Jordan.' She gave the boy a wave, before savouring the warm touch of Nick's arm through hers, and stepped out through the external doors. 'I felt a bit superfluous in there.'

'It was a simple suturing job and either one of us could have done it.'

'True, but I wasn't thinking about medical skills. You wanted to do the stitching and Jordan obviously wanted you to treat him.'

'Did he?' Nick looked surprised. 'I guess I've done a bit with that unit and he knows me.'

A bit? 'That would be the understatement of the day. You've done heaps with those boys in the last couple of weeks.'

The surprise on his face rolled into pleasure. 'I suppose I have but it's been fun and…' He shrugged his shoulders as if he couldn't find the right words.

'Gratifying?'

He nodded. 'Yeah, I guess it has been.'

She gave him a sideways glance, stunned that he hadn't made the connection between how he felt and the work he'd been doing at KC. 'You're really great with the boys. The way you talk to them and respect their growing independence, you're a natural.'

He cleared his throat. 'I don't know about that.'

'I do.' She spoke emphatically, the culmination of all her thoughts about him and the children unexpectedly forming into words. 'You genuinely like kids.'

He gave a wry grin. 'I guess I do.'

She smiled and hugged her secret daydream to her heart. 'Yes, you really do. I've seen you in action and you'd make a wonderful father.'

He immediately stiffened against her, his arm taut with

tension. 'There's more to being a father than being able to chat to kids.'

'Obviously.' She stopped walking and turned to face him because this time she wasn't going to back away from the topic. 'But the thing is, you seem to really love being with them.'

'I love cats too but I don't have one.' His voice developed a chilly edge. 'My parents never recovered from the blow parenthood dealt them—spending so much time caring for Sarah and then losing her so young—and my life isn't suited to fatherhood. I don't want to be a father and I don't for one minute regret the choice I made.'

She stared into his eyes long and hard, looking for a sign that belied his words. 'Really?'

A flinty hardness she hadn't seen before glinted back at her. 'Really.'

A chill spread through her at odds with the heat of the day, spiking her like jagged shards of ice. Her daydream imploded, the faces of imagined children instantly vanishing.

Nick's hands suddenly cupped her face and he brought his mouth down onto hers in a kiss that rocked her all the way down to the soles of her feet.

He pulled back, his eyes loaded with the haze of desire. 'Summer fun, remember? This isn't for ever, it's all about now.'

She dug deep, burying her pain that he had no vision of her in his future, and she unearthed her sixteen-year-old self. 'In that case, you need to win me a doll on a stick.' She ran her finger down his shirt. 'And if you do, you might just get lucky.'

He gazed down at her, his voice huskily deep. 'How lucky?'

'Shelter-shed lucky.'

He grabbed her hand and marched her toward the shooting gallery.

CHAPTER TEN

KIRBY switched on the clinic's security and slammed the door behind her, pleased the long day had finally come to a close. The heat wave meant too many sunburned tourists suffering from heatstroke and dehydration, and the evening clinic had been full. She dumped her laptop and green enviro-friendly shopping bag that held her dinner—a can of chicken korma—onto the front seat of the four-wheel drive and then slid her key into the ignition.

The engine roared into life and she pushed the gear stick into first, preparing to turn right. *Home time.* But every part of her wanted to turn left and head out to Riversleigh, head out to see Nick and spend some time lying on the cool, mossy grass surrounded by ferns. Spend time making love with him.

She gripped the wheel harder and tugged right. She would *not* be needy. It was possible to go eighteen hours without seeing him, without inhaling that complex scent of soap, fresh pine and masculinity, and without feeling his strong arms around her, cradling her close.

Possible, yes. Enjoyable, no. Her mouth curved up into a private smile as she recalled his earlier goodbye kiss when he'd left the clinic at two p.m. He'd found her in the supply room, kicked the door closed and pinned her to the wall with the gentle caress of his entire body. His heat-filled gaze, filled with raw hunger, had shot through her so hard and fast that she'd almost orgasmed on the spot. She'd never experienced such powerful emotions from a man or for a man. It was wondrous, incredible and terrifying.

But it was also make-believe and she must remember that. This was summer frivolity, a summer fling. Nothing else, and she needed to focus on that. The summer would end, Nick would return to Melbourne City to his life in A and E and the lecture circuit, and she would finish her rotation in Port and get on with her single life that involved kids in some way.

But that was the future. For now, nothing serious was allowed to dent this time with Nick and she'd learned that at the fete. She'd pushed him to acknowledge how good he was with kids and he'd frozen on her. Knowing that, she now avoided all talk of children and as a result the last three weeks had been wonderful. Who would have guessed there were so many clandestine places for a couple to make love?

That would be sex. The realistic and grounding voice instantly reminded her that love was not part of this summer pact and it never could be. This time with Nick couldn't be anything but fun because ultimately, somehow and some way, she wanted children in her life and Nick didn't. That one thing was a huge gulf between them, impossible to bridge.

She bit her lip against the tug of concern and rounded the final corner, catching sight of her tiny fisherman's cottage with its bright display of petunias, their purple and white heads waving welcomingly in the salt-laden evening sea breeze. Her stomach rolled over in pleasure. Nick's muddy truck stood parked out front.

She jumped out of the truck, grabbed her bags and opened the gate. Turbo's stocky form charged around from the side of the house, a stick in his mouth, a hopeful look in his brown eyes.

'Hey, mate, great to see you.' *Because if you're here, so is your master.* Kirby scratched the dog hard behind the ears. 'Sorry, there's not much room in my tiny garden for sticks.' She left the doleful dog and opened the front door, stepping into the blissful coolness that only a solid stone house could offer in midsummer. The pungent aroma of fresh basil immediately permeated her nostrils and her stomach growled hungrily. 'Nick?'

'I'm in the laundry.' His deep voice sounded muffled and far away.

'I don't have a laundry.' Confused and intrigued, she walked along the long central hall to the very back of the house where a lean-to had been added, probably over seventy years ago. She used it to hold her body board, bike and as a place to dry her wetsuit. Other than that it contained an old copper and a hand-turned mangle, and going by the cobwebs neither had been used to wash clothes in a very long time. Kirby, like previous tenants, spent Sundays at the laundrette.

She walked through the kitchen, passing her island bench, which groaned with fresh produce from Nick's garden. Pausing only to pop one of his plump and luscious strawberries into her mouth, she stepped down into the lean-to. 'What are you do—?' Heat roared through her.

A shirtless Nick, all golden skin and rippling muscles, with a tool belt strapped low on his hips, leaned over a shiny metal laundry trough, tightening a set of taps. Her heart hammered erratically as her breath came hard and fast. This was her fantasy, except he was real flesh and blood.

'Hey, Sherlock.' He put down his wrench and pulled her into his arms. 'You're later than I thought. Busy evening clinic?' His lips caressed her forehead as his tool belt pressed into her.

'Huge evening clinic.' She didn't care that a hammer pressed into her hip and a spanner imprinted itself on her belly. She leaned in, looping her arms around his neck, and breathed deeply. Kissing him long and lingeringly, she absorbed his taste, his touch and his boundless energy. A flash of white caught her eye and she reluctantly drew back, curiosity pushing her as she peered over his shoulder.

The old mangle and copper had vanished. Instead, a small white washing machine nestled snugly between the trough and a laminate bench, which had a power point fixed to its back board and two cupboards fitted underneath. High above the bench was an old-fashioned but very functional clothes airer suspended from the ceiling with a rope and pulley system so clothes could be aired and retrieved. Total surprise swirled through her, absorbing most coherent thought. 'What's all this?'

He turned, keeping one arm slung around her waist, his face creasing in a wide grin. 'You needed a laundry so I traded vegetables for the reconditioned machine and bartered time in Jason's joinery to make the bench against keeping Jase supplied with tomatoes so he can make his famous Port chutney.'

He stepped forward and slipped open the top drawer under the bench and a small ironing board appeared. 'What do you think?'

'I...I'm speechless. I didn't expect... I...' Words failed her as her throat tightened. No man had ever done anything so thoughtful for her in her life.

A hint of a worried frown hovered on his brow. 'You do like it?'

Words couldn't come close to describing how she really felt so she kissed him hard and fast, hoping she wouldn't cry on the spot. She pulled back, breathless. 'I love it. Thank you. I can't believe you did this.'

He undid the tool belt, laying it on the bench, and then pulled on his shirt, which had been hanging behind the door. 'It's crazy for you to not have a laundry. I had a chat to the hospital board and they said if I wanted to do the work they had no objections, and you know how I enjoy working with my hands.'

She stepped in close, remembering exactly what his hands could do when they touched her body. She trailed her finger down the front of his shirt. 'I do know that and you're extremely good at it.' She couldn't keep the husky tone of desire out of her voice.

A flare of heat surged in his eyes but instead of pulling her hard against him, as she expected, he kissed her quickly on the cheek and grabbed her hand. 'Come on, that can wait. It's eight o'clock and I know you won't have eaten. I've got organic chicken with pesto and a home-grown salad all ready and waiting.'

She pulled against his hand, glancing over at the bench. 'What happened to being carefree, irresponsible and sixteen?'

His lips curved into a crooked smile. 'We've been sixteen a lot lately and right now I'm hankering for some long, lazy loving in a bed after a healthy meal.'

She stepped up against him. 'A bed? You're sounding like an old fuddy-duddy.'

His brown brows rose as his hands gently gripped her shoulders to keep a slight distance between them. 'No dessert for you until you've eaten all your veggies.'

'Is that a promise?'

'Absolutely.' The word sounded strangled as he moved toward the door, tugging her behind him in the direction of the kitchen.

She followed, surprised he hadn't wanted to christen the laundry but happy in the knowledge he wanted to have long, leisurely sex. She was totally up for a new experience.

Nick pulled the can of chicken korma out of the shopping bag and held it by the tips of his fingers as if it were poison. 'Seriously, though, you really don't take very good care of yourself, Kirby. When did you actually cook something decent to eat?'

'Hey, that has vegetables. Besides, I've been busy.' His words rankled but she appreciated where he was coming from. He'd faced a life-threatening illness and as a result treated his body with more respect than she treated hers. The horrible hot flushes that scorched her body twice a day might improve if she made sure she ate more soy and ate less processed food. 'I promise to try harder.'

'Good.' But his expression clearly showed he didn't believe her.

She poured their drinks and set the table while Nick plated up the chicken salad, enjoying the camaraderie of being in the kitchen with another person. The truth was she hated cooking for one. Hated that no matter how hard she tried she always ended up with enough food for two, hated that she had to cook *and* clean up, but most of all she hated the silence that came with the meal for one. So she ate on the hop, standing up, or with a plate balanced on her knee, watching a movie, any way that didn't scream, *You're all alone*.

But she couldn't tell Nick any of that. She refused to admit her loneliness to him—after all, he hadn't signed up for anything more than sex and fun.

He's feeding you. He built you a laundry.

Don't go there, don't read more into this than there is.

But she disregarded the warning and let the words circle her heart, sending out fine connecting threads as she sat down opposite him. 'This looks sensational, thank you.'

His eyes sparkled with warmth as he raised his freshly squeezed glass of orange juice toward her and clinked it against hers. 'It's my absolute pleasure.'

She lost herself in his gaze as she forked some of the moist chicken into her mouth, letting the flavours of garlic and basil explode against her tongue. 'This is divine. I've never tasted chicken like this before.'

He nodded slowly. 'This is one reason why I grow my own food but I won't get back on my soapbox about it again tonight.' He drizzled virgin olive oil and balsamic vinegar over his endive and smiled at her as he ate his meal.

She basked in his gaze and asked him about his plans for the farm. With his fork waving, he enthusiastically outlined his success with some of the home-made anti-insect remedies given to him by the old Italian gardeners in the nursing home.

He asked about her day, laughed with her over her story about Meryl reducing the antagonistic, skull-and-crossbones-wearing, tough motorcycle rider into a compliant, polite and slightly scared patient with the flourish of a large glass syringe. From that point their conversation roamed wide and free, taking in the politics of health, the value of popular fiction and why it generated such rancour amongst the literati, and finishing with the importance of quality coffee on a Sunday morning. Kirby adored and savoured every single moment.

Nick drained his glass, scrunched his napkin into a ball and tossed it onto his now empty plate. 'Seeing as I've taken over your kitchen tonight, how about you take over mine on Friday? I'll have been harvesting all afternoon, ready for Saturday's market, so I won't be in the mood to cook.'

Something akin to pure happiness streaked through her as she pictured herself in his warm cosy home, sitting down with him at his huge farmhouse table and sharing eclectic conversation.

Be very careful—you're not playing for keeps. 'You'd let me loose in your kitchen to play with the Aga?'

He grinned. 'I think you'd be a perfect match for my kitchen.'

Perfect match. Recipes spun through her head as miniature castles rose slowly in the background of her mind. 'I'll ask Gaz to get me some prawns, mussels and calamari so I can make us paella. How does that sound?'

He stood up, walked around the table and pulled her to her feet. Gazing straight at her, a smouldering look in his eye, he spoke softly, his breath stroking her cheek. 'It sounds fine but I'm really more interested in what you have planned for tonight's dessert.'

'Let me think.' She leaned forward, nonchalantly trailing her forefinger along her bottom lip in a provocative gesture. 'Strawberries, cream and me.'

He shuddered against her and cleared his throat. 'I'll take it now but in reverse order.'

'Come with me.' Smiling, she took his hand and led him down the hall to her bedroom, glorying in the fact he wanted her so badly. She walked through the doorway, dropped his hand and slipped her dress from her shoulders. It cascaded down across her belly and pooled at her feet. She stepped out of it and turned to find him standing with his back against the closed door, his simmering gaze fixed on her.

A flush of need raced through her and instantly her breasts

tightened as her body readied itself for him. She held out her arms. 'What are you doing over there?'

'Watching you. You're totally gorgeous, do you know that?' He walked toward her and pulled the clip from her hair, sending it tumbling down around her face. 'I've wanted to do that all day.'

She tilted her head back looking up at him. 'I've dreamed of this all day.'

He buried his face in her hair and she closed her eyes, wanting to block out everything except his wondrous touch.

The next moment her feet left the floor. He lifted her into his arms and swung her around before lowering her onto the bed as if she weighed nothing more than a child. The mattress moved as he lay down next to her and she opened her eyes to find him straddling her.

He gazed down at her, his expression a mixture of desire and decisions. 'Being sixteen has been fun but I want to show you what an experienced lover with all the time in the world can do.'

She grinned up at him. 'That sounds very smug.'

A dangerous glint shimmered in his eyes. 'I doubt you'll be disappointed.'

He lowered his mouth to hers as his hands travelled to places he knew made her heart race and her body lush with wanton hunger. She lost herself in his touch, craving it like a drowning man craved air and giving in to the most exquisite sensations she'd ever experienced in her life. Opening her body and her heart, she gave herself up to him completely and utterly, letting herself freefall into the glorious abyss of wonder in a way she'd never allowed herself to do before.

Much later Kirby lay in Nick's arms, the moonlight streaming in through the uncovered window, illuminating the white sheet that covered their naked bodies. His soft breathing sounded reassuringly behind her, and his exhaled breath tickled her neck. His promise of expert loving had hit every target. Her limbs now felt like hot treacle—thick and runny and deliciously unable to support her. She couldn't keep the smile off her face.

Before tonight their coupling had been hot, frantic and edgy as if they'd both feared they might never have another chance of being in each other's arms. And the moment the sex had been over they'd gone back to their respective homes or jobs, depending on the time of day. But tonight had been totally different.

What had Nick promised? Long, lazy loving, and he'd more than delivered. Her body, so overloaded with pleasure, now relaxed into his embrace, feeling like it had come home.

It's just sex.

It's way past sex. It's a new sparkly laundry, it's delicious food and conversation, it's companionship, it's having things in common, it's… Clarity sucked the breath from her lungs as she came face to face with reality. *It's love.*

Oh, God, she loved him.

Her hands gripped her temples, as if squeezing hard would change things. Loving Nick was dumb, stupid, senseless and a one-way ticket to heartache. They wanted totally different things from their lives so how had she let this happen? How had the protective barricades around her heart melted away, leaving her vulnerable?

But how it happened wasn't really important. The fact was it *had* happened and this was her new reality.

Nick moved in his sleep, his legs entwining with hers so his body wrapped around her, cocooning her completely. What would it be like to lie like this every night?